PROPERLY HUMBLED

A Pride and Prejudice Variation Novel

APRIL FLOYD

To my readers in The Janeside, at Fanfiction dot net, and across the world — I am so very thankful for your support, kindness, and guidance.

"Unfortunately an only son (for many years an only child), I was spoilt by my parents, who, though good themselves (my father, particularly, all that was benevolent and amiable), allowed, encouraged, almost taught me to be selfish and overbearing; to care for none beyond my own family circle; to think meanly of all the rest of the world; to wish at least to think meanly of their sense and worth compared with my own. Such I was, from eight to eight and twenty; and such I might still have been but for you, dearest, loveliest Elizabeth! What do I not owe you! You taught me a lesson, hard indeed at first, but most

advantageous. By you, I was <u>properly</u> <u>humbled</u>. I came to you without a doubt of my reception. You shewed me how insufficient were all my pretensions to please a woman worthy of being pleased." - Jane Austen, Pride and Prejudice

Elizabeth Bennet stood beside her eldest sister Jane in their Uncle Gardiner's warehouse in Cheapside. They were to choose whatever trinkets they desired before joining their Aunt Madeline for an afternoon in their favorite tea shoppe near Mayfair.

Jane Bennet could not decide between a rose silk bolt that had arrived from the Far East only the day before or an intricate fan made of feathers arranged in a most ingenious pattern.

Elizabeth, being a reader, chose two novels she had not yet had the pleasure of reading. "Jane, you must decide. Aunt will soon think we have forgotten her."

Jane closed her eyes and thought of dancing with Mr. Bingley, though she knew it was a silly dream, and chose the rose silk. "A new gown would be a welcome luxury in London in the springtime."

Elizabeth raised a brow at her lovely sister. Jane Bennet could go about Town in a plain muslin day dress and still turn the heads of many a gentleman.

The only one she cared for was Mr. Charles Bingley, though Elizabeth did not believe Mr. Bingley deserved her sister's consideration. He followed behind his meddling sisters and his ear was ever bent to their bothersome advice, and that of one Mr. Fitzwilliam Darcy. Elizabeth held tighter to her books and would not allow herself to wander into such unhappy thoughts on a rare lovely day in London.

Moving closer to Jane, she fingered the edge of the silk bolt. "Aunt Madeline's friend Mrs. Westings shall host a ball in the weeks after Easter. Perhaps there will be time enough to have a new dress made before then?"

Jane followed Elizabeth to their Uncle Gardiner's office. "I had not thought of any ball in particular, Lizzy, only that the color is quite lovely against my skin."

Elizabeth knew her sister did consider a ball in particular. It was the one that Mrs. Hurst, the sister of Charles and Caroline Bingley, was to give just before the summer when all the families of the Ton would migrate to their country estates.

Instead of divulging her knowledge of Jane's aspirations for that ball, Elizabeth placed her books on Edward Gardiner's desk. "Jane and I have chosen Uncle, but we must return home to gather Aunt Madeline before setting off to Hanford's for tea."

Uncle Gardiner waved a hand to his assistant and had the man wrap Elizabeth and Jane's selections. He would have them delivered to his townhouse later in the day. "Lizzy, you never choose silk as Jane does. Surely you might fancy a new dress as well?"

Elizabeth smiled at her uncle. "I have more dresses than any young woman needs, sir. Books, well, there may never be too many at hand. Besides, I shall be in Kent for Easter and books will be of more use than a lovely bolt of silk."

Jane began to doubt her choice just as she doubted Mr. Bingley. "I ought to have chosen the fan. I have never seen such a lovely thing in all my life."

Waving his nieces away as a fellow tradesman appeared at his office door, Edward Gardiner was not surprised by Elizabeth's choices. She had always been studious and inquisitive and Fanny Bennet, his sister, had never doted on her second daughter the same as she did Jane.

Jane Bennet, being the fairest of her sisters, was to marry well due to the entailment on Longbourn, the Bennet home near Meryton. Mrs. Bennet had hopes that by sending Jane to Town after Mr. Bingley a match with the man might still be made.

Edward Gardiner had thought to write to his brother and sister Bennet and express how little regard he held for any young man who would leave Jane without an offer of marriage, but he knew his opinion would not matter much.

He watched his nieces as they hurried from his warehouse before returning his attention to his business.

In the carriage that rolled quickly towards the Gardiner townhouse, Elizabeth watched her sister as the pale beauty glanced out upon the street. "Miss Bingley will surely send an invitation to her ball if you write her and say you are in Town?"

Jane turned and gave a timid smile. "I had thought to write her this afternoon. Do you believe it would be too forward?"

Elizabeth shook her head and patted Jane's hand. Though she did not believe the Bingley sisters would be eager for her sister's company, Elizabeth smiled and attempted to reassure Jane. "I am certain she will reply and offer an invitation. How could she not?"

The carriage halted before the Gardiner town-house and the footman went to the door to retrieve Mrs. Gardiner, for she was awaiting the return of her nieces.

Moments later, Aunt Madeline settled in the carriage and Jane moved from her bench to sit beside Elizabeth. The sisters were eager to visit their favorite tea shoppe with their aunt. She had introduced them to the establishment years ago and it was tradition they visit at least once whenever they were in Town.

When the carriage pulled away from the town-house, Jane spoke of her difficulty in choosing from the many trinkets and treasures in their uncle's ware-house. "I cannot believe I did not choose that fan. 'Twas a lovely blue, nearly the shade of my eyes. But the rose silk will make a lovely ball gown don't you think Lizzy?"

Elizabeth nodded. "Uncle may have the fan sent with the silk, Jane. He likes to surprise us, you know."

Aunt Madeline cleared her throat and the girls grew silent. "There is much more use to be had from the silk, Jane. A fan is a lovely accessory, to be sure. Shall we visit the modiste on the morrow?"

Jane clapped her hands and grew excited over this plan. "Oh, Aunt, could we? There is nothing in Meryton to compare."

Mrs. Gardiner turned to Elizabeth. "Lizzy, will you join us?"

Elizabeth sighed and shook her head in reply. "I would not. I must make ready for my trip to Kent to visit Charlotte."

The carriage stopped outside their favorite tea shoppe and the sisters became excited for the hour they would spend in the quaint establishment.

Jane stood still for a moment admiring the front of the shoppe. "Mother and the younger girls would so love this place but I only wish to come with you and Lizzy."

Their Aunt Madeline agreed. "Your mother and sisters have their own diversions in Hertfordshire when you are away and so we must not worry on their account."

The ladies made their way into the shoppe that was neat as a pin. The tables were covered in fine, white linen and the aroma of cakes and scones scented the air while the intoxicating spice of a host of teas lent to the rich ambience of the elegant shoppe.

Taking a table near the front window, the Gardiner party of three sat and spoke happily with the proprietor. "Mr. Hanford," said Madeline Gardiner, "how lovely to see you once more. We shall have our usual if it pleases you."

The elderly gentleman nodded and remarked to Elizabeth and Jane. "Has it been a year since last we met? I declare, the Bennet sisters lend such merriment to my humble shoppe."

Jane gave the gentleman her most beautiful smile and thanked him for his kind words. "Sir, my sister and I are honored to sit in the finest tea shoppe in all of London and command your attention. 'Tis the happiest tradition of our existence!"

Mr. Hanford gave a small bow before moving away to speak to a pair of ladies who had just entered. A shadow crossed Elizabeth's face as she saw the women he spoke with were none other than Miss Bingley and her sister Mrs. Hurst.

Elbowing Jane gently and inclining her head towards the door, Elizabeth shifted her eyes in their direction without turning her head.

Jane took her sister's cue and glanced slowly towards the door. Unlike Elizabeth, her face displayed a welcoming smile as she watched the Bingley party move to a table not far from their own. "Lizzy, perhaps I might speak with Miss Bingley now and save myself the trouble of writing her?"

Elizabeth would not dissuade Jane from her plan though she wished Miss Bingley had not appeared to cast a shadow on their visit to Mr. Hanford's shoppe. "Do go speak with her Jane and give my regards."

Jane rose and smoothed her skirts as she turned her gaze to the ladies of the Bingley table. Leaving her reticule on her seat, Jane moved confidently among the empty chairs until she stood beside the ladies Elizabeth simply abhorred.

Mr. Bingley's sisters were snobbish and too fond of their own opinions by half, but Jane Bennet was an amiable young lady who rarely focused on the faults of others. It was the reason she and Charles Bingley had been so attracted the first night they met at the assembly in Meryton.

Miss Bingley had seen Jane approaching and her face formed into what passed for polite interest in Town. Mrs. Hurst looked up as Jane appeared and quickly glanced to her sister, smiling with a warmth that did not reach her light green eyes. "Why Miss Bennet how lovely to see you once more! We did not know you were in Town."

Jane allowed her nervous hands to rest at her sides and attempted to quell the butterflies in her stomach. Mr. Bingley's sisters had been kind to her before but she did not think for a moment that Louisa Hurst was happy to see her now.

Caroline sat up straighter upon seeing Jane would not leave and offered her a seat at their table. "Miss Bennet, how long are you to be in Town?"

"Several months I should think. Elizabeth will be leaving for Kent soon. Her best friend Charlotte Lucas married our cousin Mr. Collins and has sent for Lizzy to come for a visit over Easter."

Louisa raised a brow and nodded. "Tis a shame we shall not be in Town much longer, either. Charles has accepted an invitation from Mr. Darcy to spend the summer at Pemberley but we do have a few social events on our calendar before then. I would extend an invitation to our ball, Miss Bennet, but the guest list is already larger than we anticipated. I hope you understand."

Jane knew by the smile that appeared on Miss Bingley's face that Mrs. Hurst had just invented that particular story and was only being sociable while dashing her hopes of attending the ball.

Not wishing to sit with them a moment longer knowing she would never be invited to their ball,

Jane stood abruptly. "I understand, Mrs. Hurst. I am certain you have many friends in Town and I am merely an acquaintance. Forgive me, but I must be getting back to my family."

The Bingley sisters were pleased she had not made a fuss and smiled prettily as Jane nodded to them both.

Elizabeth looked up as Jane approached and cast a wary eye to the Bingley table. The sisters were smirking and whispering while glancing at Jane's retreating back. Aunt Madeline took the hand Elizabeth rested on the table to capture her attention. "Look away, Lizzy. We shall not return their unkindness."

Knowing her Aunt was correct, but irritated by the evil sisters, Elizabeth focused her eyes on Jane. Her serene expression exasperated Elizabeth and she breathed deeply to maintain her composure.

As Jane took her seat once more, Elizabeth smiled and pointed to a framed watercolor on the wall behind their table. "Look Jane, 'tis not half as lovely as your paintings. I do think your work would be quite lovely in Mr. Hanford's shoppe."

Jane Bennet was not as docile as her appearance might suggest and she made a dismissive sound in her throat. "Lizzy, be serious! What use would a man like Mr. Hanford have for the work of an amateur? I am perfectly fine. There is no need to patronize me on account of those boorish Bingley sisters."

Aunt Madeline gasped at Jane's stridently whispered words and glanced at Elizabeth wondering what she might think of her sister's rare display of temper. Jane was not often short with Elizabeth but in this instance, it was likely for the best.

"Oh Jane, I was not patronizing you. Your paintings are lovelier than any of these," Elizabeth said, her voice faltering as she pretended to be terribly interested in the watercolors.

Their most anticipated visit to Hanford's continued in a subdued fashion after the exchange, but Elizabeth found she could not enjoy their surroundings until the Bingley sisters rose and quit the shoppe three quarters of an hour later.

CHAPTER 2

ON THE WAY to Cheapside in their carriage, Elizabeth had grown pensive while her aunt and sister discussed the Bingley sisters and their plans for the summer months. She had not been attending and so was surprised by Jane's question.

"Isn't Pemberley near Lambton, Lizzy? Mr. Darcy did mention it once I believe, when I was sick at Netherfield."

Elizabeth nodded at Jane's question. "It is," she said and turned to their aunt. "Do you recall Pemberley from your time in Lambton, Aunt?"

Madeline Gardiner's face fairly beamed with the beautiful smile that formed on her lips at the memory. "I do, Lizzy. I recall visiting the estate with my own mother many years ago when old Mr. Darcy would open the grounds for Founder's Day. What grand picnics were given around the lake, why you cannot imagine! You must experience it once if you are there in the summer, that is if Mr. Darcy has continued the tradition."

Elizabeth knew she would love to attend just such an event but was not certain she would enjoy seeing Mr. Darcy again. Their acquaintance was quite odd when she thought of it. They had each given offense to the other but during Jane's illness, and subsequent meetings before his party departed Hertfordshire for London, Elizabeth had come to believe that perhaps there was something of a mutual respect between them.

Except for the fact of Mr. Darcy's interference in Jane's happiness and the story Mr. Wickham had shared of the man's treachery, Elizabeth might have fancied fostering a friendship with the master of Pemberley.

In any event, she would not soon be in the Lake District. Her next travels would take her to Kent in but a week's time. "I can't imagine Mr. Darcy would ever break with tradition. Perhaps Uncle might be persuaded to travel there come the summer? Jane and I shall be happy to stay in Town with the children while you are away."

Aunt Madeline thought Elizabeth's idea was

indeed a good one. "I shall speak to him of it at dinner tonight. I have wished to visit Lambton for some time. Summer in Town is simply unbearable."

The Gardiner carriage arrived again at Gracechurch Street and Elizabeth waited until her sister and aunt were free of the conveyance. It was a lovely afternoon and she dreaded sitting in the parlor, though the Gardiner townhouse was perfectly situated to capture the afternoon sun.

At the door, she spoke of her wish to wander the park across the way before succumbing to the somnolent atmosphere of the sun-drenched parlor. "Aunt Madeline, I would walk for a time if it pleases you."

Jane agreed when Elizabeth begged her to come along and the two ladies joined arms before stepping toward the street. A young maid their Aunt had called to join them from inside the townhouse came lagging behind moments later.

Once inside the park, Elizabeth led Jane to a path that circled a small lake and breathed deeply of the air that was much fresher than could be found in the crowded streets of London.

Jane was quiet, waiting for her sister to speak. That was the usual way of their relationship. Jane was the amiable yet quiet sister whose serenity in

every situation highlighted Elizabeth's happy, spir-
ited nature.

Their mother, Francine Bennet, was prone to
bouts of nerves and anyone who knew the Bennet
sisters also knew that the elder two were the most
even in temperament with the younger two being
replicas of their mother.

Yet, in comparison to the quiet Jane, the fire of
Mrs. Bennet's mercurial nature lent a spark to Elizabeth's own personality that could not be otherwise
explained.

Only the middle sister, Mary, preferred the soli-
tude of her room as assiduously as Mr. Bennet
sought his study. It was here any resemblance ended,
for Mary was a pious young lady far more serious in
temperament. Mr. Bennet made sport of one and all,
friend and neighbor alike.

Elizabeth owned a greater share of her father's
temperament. She and Mr. Bennet were of a like
mind when seen together in his study reading or
when at the dinner table tormenting their family
members with rapier wit and sarcasm.

In London, Elizabeth had become pensive and
Jane wondered at the change. Instead of waiting
until they were returned to the Gardiner townhouse,
Jane voiced her concern. "Lizzy, I am pleased you

have come to London for I am never very happy when we are apart, but you are much too sad lately."

Elizabeth had known Jane would notice her melancholy, though she tried not to dwell on her own unhappiness over Mr. Darcy. "I am not sad, Jane. I am still your loving sister who would not be parted for long from your side. If there is any lack of happiness on my part, it is because of the Bingleys and how you have been mistreated for their amusement."

Jane took Elizabeth's hand as they followed the curving path before them. "There is no need for sorrow on that score, Lizzy. Mr. Bingley is undecided and thus easily swayed by his sisters and friends. If he desires to know me better, I am here. But I am not pining for him. I want a man who cannot breathe without me by his side, don't you?"

Elizabeth was surprised by Jane's candor. Her sweet, sincere sister had never spoken quite this way and it heartened Elizabeth to hear her words. "Indeed, Jane, you've said it perfectly. What use is a man whose affections are so easily changed?"

"Mr. Bingley may yet surprise us, Lizzy, but I will not allow myself to hope for more without good reason."

Astonished by her sister's sentiment, Elizabeth halted her steps. "I cannot believe these words are falling from your lips, Jane Bennet. I thought you were in love with Mr. Bingley all this time."

Jane's bottom lip trembled with emotion. "I might have been once upon a time, Lizzy. But I must guard my heart against foolish disappointment. To hope for a thing that may never be is too painful to bear twice."

Elizabeth's anger at the Bingley sisters grew in that moment. What right had they to interfere in Jane's happiness? Jane Bennet was the loveliest lady Mr. Bingley was ever likely to meet, a perfect match to his sunny disposition if not his fickle nature.

How she longed to take Jane to Kent with her instead of leaving her in Town with the very persons responsible for her current suffering. She thought she might persuade her sister to join her in the Lucas carriage on the journey to the parsonage. "Jane, perhaps you would be better served to come with me to Kent. Charlotte would not mind at all for she did always prefer your company if I was not at home."

Knowing her sister's thoughts, Jane took Elizabeth's arm in her own again and set them to continuing their walk about the lake. "I would not, Lizzy. Aunt Madeline is increasing, as you know, and I am happy to be a help to her. Mr. Bingley may do as he pleases and I shall not worry and neither shall you."

Elizabeth blew out a breath and wished to stomp her feet and throw a fit. But Jane would not be deterred as such actions in their girlhood days had never been met with capitulation. "I could delay my departure. Father gave me a nice sum when I left Longbourn, enough to take a post chaise from here to Kent."

Jane shook her head. "You will do no such thing, Lizzy. Sir William and Maria have planned to stop in London on their way to Kent and you must not inconvenience them."

Her sister spoke the truth but it frustrated Elizabeth. Yet there was nothing to be done. "You must promise to write me, Jane. I wish to know all that happens while I am away."

Jane knew she must agree if Elizabeth was to leave without delay. "I promise to write while you are gone even though there shall be very little to tell."

"I hope that your letters will inform me that Mr. Bingley has come to his senses and given a proposal, though the thought of calling Miss Bingley sister makes me quite ill."

Jane made a face and the sisters laughed merrily as they continued their walk about the lake.

CHAPTER 3

ELIZABETH SAT on the bed she shared with Jane upstairs in the Gardiner townhouse and watched as her sister made certain her small trunk was ready for the trip to Kent. "Come here and sit with me, Jane. There is nothing more that will fit in that trunk and I shall return in but a few weeks."

Jane dropped the lid gently and made certain the clasps were tightly closed. "You must behave at Rosings, Lizzy. And wear your best dresses when meeting Lady Catherine de Bourgh. From our cousin's description of the lady when he came to Longbourn, I would not wish to be in your shoes."

Elizabeth tried in vain to portray a serious aspect as Jane joined her on the bed. "I promise to behave as a proper lady and listen carefully to her pronouncements and advice lest dear Charlotte suffer for the sin of being my dearest friend."

Satisfied by her sister's pledge though certain she was not at all serious, Jane began fiddling with Elizabeth's hair brushing aside a stray curl.

A maid knocked and entered the room. "Miss, the Lucas family has arrived. There is a footman in the hall ready to take your trunk down."

The Bennet sisters stood and Jane took Elizabeth's hand. "Come Lizzy, we must go down and have tea with our dear neighbors from Hertfordshire before you continue on to Kent with them."

The sisters stood aside in the hallway as Sir William's footman hauled Elizabeth's small trunk from the room and hoisted it up on one broad shoulder. The maid dropped her eyes and blushed as the man passed and Elizabeth hid a smirk at having caught the young woman in her moment of weakness.

The footman was a handsome fellow and not the least bit ashamed of his strapping physique. Elizabeth knew he served several purposes for the Lucas family as they employed but a few servants.

As the maid followed the footman downstairs, Elizabeth motioned to the young woman's back.

"Someone finds Cedric to be most appealing," she whispered to Jane.

Jane stifled a round of giggles and gave her sister a sobering look. "Lizzy, hush now. Surely you know Cedric is admired by many young maids in Hertfordshire."

Taking her sister's hand and stepping lightly upon the first stair, Elizabeth obeyed Jane's words. It seemed her mind was forever matchmaking for others. She was not an incurable romantic but the idea of fitting two people together appealed to her adventurous nature.

Thinking again that she ought to stay behind with Jane for yet another week, Elizabeth reluctantly turned toward the parlor when she and Jane gained the entryway.

"I am certain Sir William would not mind if I were to tarry in London a bit longer, Jane."

Jane pulled her sister's hand leading her toward the parlor door. "Lizzy you will not delay your travels, not on my account. I think perhaps you are nervous to meet Cousin Collins again."

Elizabeth planted her feet, causing Jane to stumble a bit, and shook her head. "I have no fear of the man but that does not mean I wish to spend hours in his presence listening to his tedious proclamations."

Jane was immediately sorry for her tease. "You should not have to worry on that count. Our cousin shall bend Sir William's ear mercilessly. Being Charlotte's dear papa and a gentleman, Sir William will surely oblige."

Softened in her attitude by Jane's words, Elizabeth reluctantly followed her sister into the parlor. She did wish to visit Charlotte, for she was Elizabeth's dearest friend. But Jane was her sister. Knowing she must go to Kent with the Lucas party, Elizabeth resolved to accept her fate.

Jane would write her, and Aunt Madeline gave better advice on matters of the heart than she, and so Elizabeth placed a happy smile on her face as she entered the parlor to greet Sir William and Maria Lucas.

☙❧

THE TRIP to Hunsford was an enjoyable journey and Elizabeth found the time had passed too quickly once they arrived and settled at the parson's cottage.

With Sir William and Maria along to command her friend's attention, Elizabeth was given the freedom to explore the grounds of Rosings. The property was immense. Much larger than even Netherfield.

There were streams and brooks aplenty where she knew she would sit in the afternoons and enjoy a few sunny days. Spring had arrived but the chill of winter sent her feet back towards the cottage much sooner than she might have hoped and made her worry that sunny days might not be plentiful on this visit.

On the third day after their arrival, Mr. Collins announced that they would dine at Rosings with Lady Catherine and her daughter Anne de Bourgh come the evening. Charlotte had told both Elizabeth and Maria of Miss de Bourgh's frailty and warned them that the young mistress might leave them after dinner for her bedchamber. "She is a lovely young lady but not suited for long evenings in the parlor. Lady Catherine says that she and Mr. Darcy will marry one day but I rather doubt it. How will she provide him an heir in her state?"

Elizabeth found satisfaction in imagining Mr. Darcy married to such a young woman as he was not one for idle conversation and had never seemed comfortable when in the company of others. They would be a perfect match.

When their carriage arrived at the front of Rosings that evening, Elizabeth thought she had never seen such a lovely home. The stones held a rich, buttery patina that glowed in the waning light of the evening and the greenery around the front drive was meticulously maintained.

Though there had been plenty to interest her on their trip from London, the sight of Rosings provided such a visual bounty Elizabeth caught her breath. She was enamored with grand homes and their grounds and had spent a good deal of time dreaming she was the mistress of Netherfield while it stood empty for many years before Mr. Bingley came to let the property.

She knew the moment she was back in London with Jane, she would likewise daydream of Rosings. It might prove more difficult since the de Bourgh family inhabited the home but Elizabeth Bennet was a bit of a dreamer at heart.

Following behind Charlotte and Mr. Collins, happily escorted on one arm by Sir William, Elizabeth easily climbed the broad stone steps and waited as a butler welcomed them inside.

In the parlor before dinner, Elizabeth sat and listened patiently to the questions of Lady Catherine. "Miss Bennet, Mr. Collins has informed me that your father never saw fit to employ a governess. With five daughters, I must say I cannot see the sense of such folly. What have you to say for yourself, young lady?"

Elizabeth had not expected the lady to take such an interest in her life but she recalled Mr. Collins had been quite adamant that his patroness wished him to marry from among her sisters. "Your ladyship, my father believed he might do as well as any governess. Why he took it upon himself to make fine readers of us all though Mother did her best to see that we could stitch and paint screens."

Lady Catherine squinted at the impertinent girl and gave a slight shake of her head. "I would not presume to know why you would admit to having such a foolish father, Miss Bennet. 'Tis not surprising as Mr. Collins has regaled us many a time since his return to Hunsford with tales of your own foolish behavior. Have any other offers of marriage upon which to rely that gave you the courage to dash the hopes of your family?"

Elizabeth bit the inside of her cheek and forced away the laughter that rose in her throat. The woman was positively vulgar, rude, and without an ounce of the breeding one would expect from a peer. "I have none, your ladyship, and desire none. I am but one and twenty with an older sister above me still at home."

Lady Catherine saw that she could not ruffle the feathers of the young lady and turned to Mr. and Mrs. Collins to engage them in another of her endless tales of benevolence and superiority.

Anne de Bourgh sat quietly observing the interactions in the parlor but met Elizabeth's gaze without looking away.

While Lady Catherine was busy pontificating over the proper way to discipline servants, Elizabeth surreptitiously moved to sit closer to the young mistress. "Tis a lovely home you have, Miss de Bourgh. I am pleased to make your acquaintance."

The young lady gave Elizabeth a beautiful smile before glancing to her mother to be certain the woman's attention settled on their remaining guests. "Likewise, Miss Elizabeth, it is not often young ladies of my age visit Rosings. Shall you stay for very long? Mrs. Collins has said you are a great friend. I must admit her excitement in anticipating your arrival did infect me as well."

Until dinner was announced, Elizabeth remained in conversation with Miss de Bourgh as the rest of her party carried on with listening to Lady Catherine and agreeing with her every word.

And so it was a friendship began between Elizabeth Bennet and Anne de Bourgh. After dinner, and before her party returned home, Elizabeth was pleased that the young woman remained in the parlor in spite of her mother's admonition to retire upstairs. They found very much in common, not the least being their mutual love of books.

As the Collins party said their farewells at the front door of Rosings, Elizabeth whispered to her new friend. "I shall come each day, if you wish, and read with you. I have two novels I brought from London that we might enjoy."

Anne was most pleased and advised Elizabeth to come each day before tea. "Mother will not mind, for she is often busy in her study when we are without visitors."

Later in the evening, once they were all returned to the cottage, Elizabeth retrieved her novels and left them on the small table between the two beds in the room she shared with Maria Lucas so that she might remember to take them to Rosings.

๛

At the end of the next week, Sir William and Maria left Kent for Hertfordshire but Elizabeth remained with the Collins's as she found Charlotte and Miss Anne's company quite enjoyable.

The morning after the Lucas family had gone, Elizabeth woke early and left the cottage with nothing more than a warm scone in hand and her spencer to guard against the chill morning air. She was eager to walk about before accompanying Charlotte to Rosings for their usual visit with Miss Anne.

Turning in the lane towards the grand home, Elizabeth thought she might admire the house from afar before making her way into Hunsford. She recalled that she wished to visit the shoppes in town to see if there was some trinket she might find for Jane before returning to London.

In less than an hour, Elizabeth stood outside a shoppe that displayed an assortment of ribbons and lace that was the finest she had seen in some time. She decided to take a look inside before returning to the cottage.

As she made to enter the shoppe, a carriage

passed and she recognized the monogram on the door. She and Jane had seen the man, with a young lady who must be his sister, in Town in the grand conveyance once in Mayfair.

Her heart fluttered in her chest when she caught a glimpse of his profile. It was Mr. Darcy! Turning quickly away, Elizabeth scooted into the shoppe and hurried to the rear of the establishment.

She had known Mr. Darcy would come to Rosings, for Charlotte had said as much before her father and Maria left. Irritated that he was now present, Elizabeth lingered in the shoppe in an effort to avoid the man.

Grabbing a spool of ribbon that was Jane's favorite shade of green, Elizabeth walked to the counter and asked for a lengthy portion to be cut as she opened her reticule. Her mind was racing to fix upon a plan of action to leave the town unnoticed.

She would make her way to the other end of Hunsford and walk through the woods to return to her cousin's cottage rather than risk walking back the way she had come and encountering Mr. Darcy near Rosings.

Happy with her solution, Elizabeth paid for the ribbon and tucked the small paper package inside her reticule. As she followed another young lady to the door, she halted as the woman left the shoppe.

Allowing herself a moment to peer into the street before stepping outside, Elizabeth drew in a breath to steady her nerves. There was no sign of Mr. Darcy's carriage.

Recalling that she must go with Charlotte to Rosings that afternoon, Elizabeth tried to think of how she might stay behind at the cottage instead.

Charlotte would not press her if she said her head hurt and she could easily pretend recovery once her friend returned home. Pleased with her forethought, Elizabeth walked happily through Hunsford knowing she would not have to meet Mr. Darcy that particular day.

When she arrived at the cottage, Mr. Collins was leaving to tend his parishioners and Charlotte was standing by the door waving to him. "We shall be leaving soon for Rosings, husband. Here is Elizabeth now."

Mr. Collins tipped his hat as the small gig, one that Miss Anne used from time to time, moved off down the lane.

The fine conveyance could never have been afforded by Mr. Collins and Elizabeth knew that Lady Catherine only allowed his use of it for official duties. The man had to walk to Rosings each morning before breaking his fast and retrieve the equipage. After luncheon, he would return the gig to the stables of Rosings and repeat the process the following day.

Elizabeth opened the gate and remembered her plan to feign a headache. She shielded her eyes as if the sun hurt them and walked slowly to the door. "I fear I am not well this morning Charlotte. I have a terrible headache and would prefer to lie down for a time. Please give my regards to Miss Anne, for I did so wish to visit with her today."

Charlotte took Elizabeth's hand and led her inside the cottage. Taking her friend's spencer, she walked Elizabeth to the stairs. "Lizzy, I have some herbs in the storeroom that might ease your pain. Would you like for me to get them for you?"

Elizabeth embraced her friend, feeling a terrible guilt at worrying the woman. "I think I shall be fine after a while, Charlotte. Please do not be concerned. If I am not recovered by the time you return home, then you may dose me as you see fit."

When at last she was alone in her room, Elizabeth waited until she was certain her friend had left the cottage before she retrieved a book Miss Anne had loaned her from the library at Rosings.

Happy that she would not have to meet with Mr. Darcy that day, Elizabeth sat by the open window enjoying the light breeze that ruffled the curtains and read for hours. Once in a while, she chastised herself for lying to Charlotte and enjoying her time alone.

CHAPTER 4

IN THE AFTERNOON, Elizabeth refreshed her appearance and went downstairs to await the Collins's return from Rosings. Her stomach registered its dissatisfaction at her decision to forego luncheon. Dinner was hours away but perhaps Charlotte would have tea served when she arrived home.

In the parlor, Elizabeth again admired the skill with which her friend had decorated the humble room. It was not as large as the parlor at Lucas Lodge but the fine furnishings handed down from Rosings more than made up for that deficiency.

Charlotte had made good use of the natural light in the room by using drapery that was not as heavy as what might be found in grander homes. All in all, the room was bright and cheerful and Elizabeth found she enjoyed it even when her cousin sat with them of an evening after dinner.

The room was not situated near the front of the cottage and at first, Elizabeth had found it strange. But after spending a fortnight with the Collins's she came to understand better.

Her cousin's study looked out up on the lane and so held the most appeal. Charlotte had wisely set up her parlor in a way that did not consider Mr. Collins's sensibilities. He much preferred the vantage point of his study where he could know the comings and goings of their neighbors.

Mr. Collins had been happy to greet Elizabeth when she arrived at Hunsford with the Lucas family and had been grudgingly civil in their ensuing conversations. His manner was softened but his words were as pompous as she recalled.

Elizabeth's refusal of the man's proposal when he first came to Longbourn had made her mother quite ill until she sought her rooms to soothe her nerves. Mr. Bennet had only smiled serenely upon finding his favorite daughter would not marry the foolish parson. With the entailment over Longbourn, such a reaction from her father made little sense to Elizabeth at the time but she was simply too pleased to have escaped a lifetime with Mr. Collins.

Interrupted in her recollections by voices in the entry, Elizabeth left the solitary attitude of the parlor to greet her returning family. Charlotte bustled through the front door in a state of excitement. Upon seeing her friend, she allowed a small crease of worry to mar her brow. "Lizzy, are you well? Mr. Darcy has come to visit with his cousin, Colonel Fitzwilliam. Isn't it a lovely surprise?"

Keeping her gaze on Charlotte, Elizabeth pretended at delight. "Indeed! I had not known Mr. Darcy was in Kent."

The ease with which she told her second lie that day was mortifying but Elizabeth would not admit to having seen his carriage earlier in Hunsford and certainly not to avoiding him at all costs.

Mr. Collins entered behind Charlotte, his countenance nearly as radiant as his wife's though he was far more excited. He stood aside for Mr. Darcy and Colonel Fitzwilliam to enter. "Welcome gentlemen, Mrs. Collins and I are most honored to have you visit our humble home this day."

Charlotte turned away from Elizabeth and addressed her most esteemed guest. "Mr. Darcy, thank you for giving us a ride home in your carriage. I shall have the maid prepare tea for our visit in the parlor."

Elizabeth found herself left abruptly alone with the men as Charlotte hurried to the kitchen. She swallowed her growing unease and spoke slowly to the man she wished least to ever meet again. "Mr. Darcy, how strange to meet you in Kent after all this time."

Mr. Darcy merely held her gaze in a most disconcerting manner and Elizabeth wished she might turn and flee to the kitchen where Charlotte had gone only moments before.

After an awkward moment, Mr. Darcy spoke. "Miss Elizabeth, 'tis a pleasure to be in your company once more."

Mr. Collins grinned widely as he stood looking to Mr. Darcy. It was plain he was nearly bursting to make the introduction of the Colonel to his cousin.

Mr. Darcy schooled his face but not before Elizabeth caught a glimpse of the irritation that passed quickly away. If there was one opinion she might share with Mr. Darcy, it was an exasperation with William Collins.

She found herself watching his lips as he spoke and forced her eyes to his cousin's face as the heat rose in her cheeks. "Colonel Fitzwilliam this is Elizabeth Bennet. She is a dear friend of Mrs. Collins from Hertfordshire."

Colonel Fitzwilliam bowed in a charming manner and Elizabeth noted the striking difference in his demeanor from that of his cousin. "I am pleased to make your acquaintance at last Miss Bennet. Darcy has regaled me with tales of his visit to Netherfield in which you featured quite prominently."

Elizabeth knew the color in her cheeks deepened further at his admission, so unexpected it was and quite bothersome. What on earth had Mr. Darcy said to the man regarding herself and her family?

Hoping her voice would not tremble, she finally replied. "Colonel, you may call me Miss Elizabeth as Miss Bennet is my eldest sister. I am delighted to make your acquaintance. Will you be in Kent for some time?"

Richard Fitzwilliam immediately saw the reason Darcy had been unable to cease his praise of Miss Elizabeth Bennet. Her eyes were bright and her smile genuine though she seemed a bit uncomfortable at present. She was a gentlewoman in her speech and manners though Mr. Collins had told them of the situation with Longbourn when speaking about his marriage to Mrs. Collins. "I believe a fortnight shall suffice, Miss Elizabeth.

Darcy and I make the trip each spring and have never stayed longer."

Elizabeth managed a smile at his answer though her mind vexed her with how she might avoid Mr. Darcy for that length of time.

When her cousin began to wax eloquent upon their good fortune at having such favored guests, Elizabeth turned and led the way to the parlor. Charlotte came shortly after, pleased as ever to have such esteemed guests in her home.

When tea arrived, Elizabeth did not have to pretend at an interest in the various cakes as her mouth watered at the sight of food. Foregoing luncheon now proved advantageous as she busied herself with surreptitious bites of seed cake instead of engaging in conversation.

Mr. Collins, a man without a thought for silence and reflection when in the company of his betters, kept his guest's attention and for that Elizabeth was most grateful.

She had to swallow the laughter that bubbled in her throat at the irony of the situation. Many had been the time when she would rather perform the most odious of tasks than be subjected to her cousin's flowery speech.

Mr. Darcy remained silent throughout the visit

but Elizabeth caught his gaze upon her on several occasions and thought he must be quite mad to seek her attention. Before she might turn away at one particular instance, he spoke and startled her into replying. "Miss Elizabeth, how is your family?"

She thought on his question for a moment wondering if his concern was genuine. Deciding he was only attempting to seem interested, for he had not said more than two words the entire time, Elizabeth allowed her lips to form a tight smile. "They were well the last I was home, Mr. Darcy. Jane is in London and I shall return there when my visit here has ended. Have you not seen my sister in Town?"

Elizabeth knew he had not but refused to resist the temptation to speak of Jane to the man she considered partially responsible for Mr. Bingley's abandonment. In her heart, she knew the plot to separate Jane from Mr. Bingley was Miss Bingley's doing but there was no doubt Mr. Darcy had approved of the scheme.

She saw a flicker of discomfort in his eyes and waited for his reply. "I have not met Miss Bennet in Town, but I would be honored if you might bring her to Darcy House when you return to London. I am certain my sister would be pleased to make her acquaintance."

Elizabeth only nodded, wondering at his words. She did not believe for a moment that he truly wished to introduce her sister to his own but when she thought of visiting Darcy House in the next weeks her heart leapt to her throat. Did she wish to continue an acquaintance with the man when he could sit before her and pretend at concern for Jane?

Not a half hour later, Mr. Darcy and the Colonel made their farewells at the cottage door and Elizabeth found she truly did have a headache after they had gone. "Charlotte, I would bother you for those herbs. I fear my head is aching once more. Perhaps it is the weather?"

Charlotte took Elizabeth's hand and steered her to the sofa in the parlor. "Wait here, my dear, and I shall return in a moment. I say, today has been most eventful. Who would have thought I might entertain Mr. Darcy and Colonel Fitzwilliam in my very own parlor? I think you must be the reason for Mr. Darcy's eagerness to see us home this afternoon."

Elizabeth gave a puzzled look to Charlotte as her friend left the room. She had nothing to do with Mr. Darcy's interest. Of course the man would visit the parsonage. He had been made welcome at Lucas Lodge while in Hertfordshire. He was only repaying the kindness shown to him by Sir William and Lady Lucas by visiting their daughter.

She hoped he would see that his duty was done as far as the parsonage was concerned and keep to Rosings for the remainder of his visit. It was likely he would spend his time in the library there and she would not be bothered to speak with him again unless they were seated together at dinner.

❧

In the following week, Elizabeth's hopes were dashed as she found herself walking in the company of Mr. Darcy on several occasions though she had told him she preferred to walk alone hoping he might leave her to wander her preferred paths without the burden of his company.

Instead, he was her companion more often than not. He spoke sparingly, as was his habit, but Elizabeth thought he must fancy himself her friend now that Jane no longer posed a threat to his good friend Mr. Bingley.

Several letters from London arrived in the weeks she had remained at Hunsford but Jane had not mentioned Mr. Bingley except for her second letter in reply to Elizabeth's inquiry on the matter.

Jane had received a letter from the Bingley sisters that revealed such meanness that had Elizabeth been in Town instead of in Kent, she would have marched to the Hurst townhouse and delivered a set down for the ages.

Caroline had said they wished to invite Jane to tea but that Mr. Bingley was involved with a young lady and seeing them together at Hurst House would only serve to make an awkward scene for all present.

The words on the letter were burned into Elizabeth's memory and she thought of them now as she walked a different path to avoid Mr. Darcy. There was only so much of the man's company she would abide graciously.

Her sister's words on the subject of Mr. Bingley caused her eyes to water but she swallowed the tears. Jane was not pining over the man and yet Elizabeth knew her sister could not possibly be pleased with her current situation.

Jane had written that she considered Mr. Bingley a gentleman regardless of his actions. She admitted she may have been mistaken to think his attention had been sincere. Her exact words tore at Elizabeth's heart as she recalled Jane's writing upon the paper.

Were he truly in love with me he would not have been persuaded to leave Hertfordshire without proclaiming himself to Father.

At last, Elizabeth felt she might accept Jane's repeated assertions regarding Mr. Bingley. Truthfully, she did not wish for Jane to be married into a family that contained the likes of the Bingley sisters. They would forever find fault with her dearest sister and make Jane's married life miserable.

Breathing deeply, Elizabeth allowed herself to release her anger with the Bingleys. Jane would fall in love and marry a man far more suitable than Mr. Bingley and she would not have to pretend to prefer the man's siblings, for she could not imagine two more detestable ladies than Caroline Bingley and Louisa Hurst.

Returning her attention to the path before her, Elizabeth stopped suddenly when she saw the figure of a man in the early morning mist approaching from the opposite direction. Dear heavens, she hoped it wasn't Mr. Darcy! Was there any place in Kent she might walk without suffering his unwanted attention?

As the man drew closer, a weight lifted from her heart when she saw it was Colonel Fitzwilliam.

She did not mind the Colonel's company in the

least, for he was a handsome and amiable man. *Not quite as handsome as Mr. Darcy*, her mind interjected and she chastised herself for such a thought. The idea made her uneasy, that she considered Mr. Darcy the handsomest man she had ever known.

The Colonel waved when he recognized her and Elizabeth waited for him on the path. "I thought you were Mr. Darcy for a moment. He seems to turn up much too often on my usual paths and so today I decided to take a different turn when leaving the parsonage."

Richard Fitzwilliam laughed heartily. "My cousin is quite fond of you Miss Elizabeth. Did you know?"

Elizabeth was surprised at his assertion. "I would not believe such a fairy tale, sir. Mr. Darcy and I did not part on the best of terms when he left Hertfordshire."

Richard offered his arm most gallantly and Elizabeth accepted. "In any case, he does admire your wit and intelligence. For a man who says very little about most people he meets, that is indeed high praise."

"Be that as it may, he is promised to Miss Anne is he not?" Elizabeth meant to make clear her decided disinterest in Mr. Darcy as anything more than an acquaintance.

Richard shrugged his shoulders. "That is our Aunt Catherine's plan I believe. Whether Darcy agrees is another matter. He is not one to take marriage lightly. He recently intervened on a friend's behalf to prevent what he considered an ill-advised match. I do not think the woman was particularly wrong for his friend but her connections left much to be desired."

Elizabeth bit her tongue as a fresh burst of irritation assaulted her senses. All this time she had thought Miss Bingley was the main instigator of the trouble between Mr. Bingley and Jane!

She would not tell the man it was her sister Mr. Darcy found unsuitable for his friend. There was no use in arguing over the situation, especially since her sister held no ill feelings for Mr. Bingley, his sisters, or Mr. Darcy. Why Jane had often defended Mr. Darcy whenever Elizabeth had spoken harshly of the man!

CHAPTER 5

AFTER A WEEK of sitting at Rosings with Miss de Bourgh and Charlotte attempting to read while keeping her ear tuned for the sound of heavy foot-steps in the hallway, Elizabeth's nerves were strained until she almost believed herself as foolish as her own mother.

She sat in the cottage parlor with Charlotte, her face quite pale, and thought of avoiding another tea at Rosings. When Mr. Collins entered the room to escort them to the carriage, Elizabeth made her excuse. "I fear I must not go and fail to be cheerful and gracious before Lady Catherine. I would not like to give offense where none is intended. Give my regards and say that I am quite sorry."

Mr. Collins's expression was one of exasperation but he could find no fault in his cousin's consideration of his patroness. "Perhaps you ought to lie down while we are away, Cousin Elizabeth. Come, Charlotte, let us not linger here and be late."

Charlotte glanced at her friend, worried that Elizabeth had seemed out of sorts since Mr. Darcy's arrival in Kent. She meant to speak to her later on the matter. To her mind, his walks in Elizabeth's company meant the man was taken with her friend no matter the complaining his habit caused Elizabeth to express after each outing.

Placing her hand on Mr. Collins's arm, Charlotte gave one last look at Elizabeth. "Dear, have some tea and ask Cook for the herbs I mixed last week. Mr. Collins is right, you ought to lie down for a time."

Elizabeth gave a weak smile to her friend and nodded as she followed them to the front door of the cottage. "I shall be well soon, Charlotte, if I follow your advice."

Once they were gone, Elizabeth asked the maid for tea and Charlotte's herbs and returned to the parlor. She was quite pleased that the room was situated so that there was no noise from passing carriages. It allowed for a quiet retreat she most desperately needed after the tedium of the prior week.

After tea was brought, Elizabeth settled in the

most comfortable chair and thought she should have brought her novel down from her room to pass the time. When she'd taken the herb concoction and drank her tea, she rose and went to retrieve her book.

Before she might gain the stairs, a knock came upon the door. She knew Cook was busy and the maid was upstairs cleaning this time of day. For a moment, she thought of ignoring the visitor but instead went to open the door.

Mr. Darcy stood patiently waiting, his hat in hand and a modest smile upon his face. Elizabeth bit back the sigh that formed on her lips and breathed deeply. Had he not realized she did not wish to be in his company? Had she not been avoiding the man at every turn?

Stepping aside, she held the door and made herself smile in a way that was not indicative of her misgivings at his appearance. "Mr. Darcy, my cousin and Charlotte are at Rosings and I was just about to go upstairs."

Elizabeth knew her manners were horrid but the Colonel's words about Mr. Darcy's interference in Jane and Mr. Bingley's relationship leapt instantly to mind when she opened the door to find him waiting on the other side.

Mr. Darcy thought to take his leave but instead

stepped over the threshold. "I would not take more than a moment of your time, Miss Elizabeth. I came to see how you were. Cousin Anne mentioned you have not seemed yourself these past few days."

Instead of turning him away, Elizabeth gathered her courage and with a sweep of her hand allowed him to enter further into the cottage. She found herself surprised at Miss de Bourgh's intuition. Saving her reflection on that news for later, she spoke as pleasantly as she might considering the circumstances. "Shall we sit in the parlor? The maid brought tea earlier."

Mr. Darcy nodded and fell into step behind her as she led him to the parlor. He was uncommonly nervous and a hair's breadth from turning and leaving instead of saying what he had come to say.

Before he might escape, Elizabeth took her seat and waited for him to do the same. Once seated with a warm cup of tea in hand, Mr. Darcy thought he may as well speak his piece as leaving now would surely seem odd.

Elizabeth, for her part, sat quietly with her tea allowing the man an opportunity to speak his mind so that she might soon be rid of him.

The tension in the room was nearly unbearable when Mr. Darcy suddenly stood and placed his cup on the table between them. He began to anxiously pace about and Elizabeth found herself not the least bit amused. What had come over the man who was ever composed and arrogant?

Deciding she would not aid him in his mission, whatever it might be, Elizabeth sat quietly pretending at more patience than she currently possessed. Her precious time alone had been curtailed to entertain an agitated Fitzwilliam Darcy.

The next moment, Elizabeth was setting her own cup down in order not to spill the remainder of its contents. Mr. Darcy had turned and rushed to her side, his face a most disturbing display of raw emotion.

As he took her now empty hands in his own, Elizabeth trembled at the warmth this connection sent through her body. She feared he had gone mad and knew it was true when he spoke.

"In vain have I struggled. It will not do. My feelings will not be repressed. You must allow me to tell you how ardently I admire and love you."

The astonishment, she thought, must surely show upon her face. In the space of but a moment, she doubted she had heard him correctly and then the heat rose from her neck and spread across her cheeks. For the life of her, Elizabeth Bennet could not form words.

Mr. Darcy, taking her reaction as encouragement, continued on. Elizabeth listened dumbfounded as he spoke about his better judgment, his connections and the inferiority of hers, and his pride at having foregone all sense and sobriety to make an offer for her hand.

Seeming quite pleased with himself, Mr. Darcy awaited her reply as though she could do nothing more than happily accept. Instead of happy tears and tender kisses, Mr. Darcy received a resounding refusal that shook him to his core and undid any composure the man possessed.

"While I ought to be grateful and most pleased by your declaration of love, I have not sought it nor have I ever desired your good opinion, sir. It would seem you have not desired mine either as your depth of feeling for me clearly brings you much pain and guilt. I am sorry to have been the cause of such suffering but I am confident you shall soon recover from your lapse in judgment."

Mr. Darcy rose at once to his feet and paced to the fireplace to lean against the mantel. His face had drained of color and Elizabeth noted the shaking of his hands. The man was altogether discomposed by her words.

He struggled for some time to regain his composure and Elizabeth merely sat silently hoping he might leave instead of continuing their awkward meeting. Instead, he whirled and ground out questions he felt she must answer. "Is that all I might expect in reply? I do wonder why, with such little attempt at civility, you have thus rejected me. Am I not a gentleman?"

Elizabeth stood, fighting every instinct to rush out of the room, and faced him. "And I might ask why with such a design to offend and insult me, you chose to tell me how you loved me against your will, your reason, and your own character. It matters little to me now, I assure you. Even if I held tender feelings for you, do you think that any consideration would tempt me to accept the man who has ruined the happiness of a most beloved sister?"

She was shocked when he smiled most heartily and gave a flippant reply. "Ah, the trouble with Miss Bennet! Indeed, I did warn Bingley against forming a match with her and am pleased with the outcome. Towards him I have been kinder than towards myself."

Elizabeth turned away, shocked by his admission. She had not expected him to readily accept blame and had been prepared to argue her point further. Instead, she caught hold of another example of his boorish behavior.

Turning to face the man, she chastised him once more. "The matter with Mr. Wickham is a terrible thing that would on its own warn me away from developing feelings of a tender nature for such a brute."

"You take an eager interest in his misfortunes, Miss Elizabeth. Why?" Mr. Darcy stood patiently awaiting further rebuke, unconcerned that his petition now lay in tatters between them never to be repaired or revisited.

Elizabeth let loose the fullness of her fury. "You reduced him to his present state of poverty. You withheld the advantages you knew to have been designed for him and yet you stand here before me behaving as though that treachery could be overlooked by a woman you dare ask give her heart into your care."

Darcy left the mantel and with quick steps crossed the room taking Elizabeth by surprise. "This is your opinion of me! I thank you for explaining it so fully. My faults are heavy indeed! But perhaps this slight list of offenses might have been overlooked, had not your pride been wounded by the truth of our disparate stations. Had I concealed my struggles and employed flattery, your bitter accusations might have been avoided. But disguise of every sort is my abhorrence. Could you expect me to rejoice in the inferiority of your connections?"

Elizabeth grew angrier with each moment that passed but held onto her composure long enough to deliver her final words to the man before leaving him standing in the parlor to see himself out. "You could not have made me the offer of your hand in any possible way that would have tempted me to accept it."

Reaching the parlor door, Elizabeth halted her steps though her feet fairly itched with the desire to escape his company. "From the very beginning of our acquaintance, your manners, your arrogance, your conceit, and your selfish disdain for the feelings of others, were sufficient to form a solid groundwork of disapproval and I had not known you a month before I felt that you were the last man in the world whom I could ever be prevailed on to marry."

Not awaiting his reply, Elizabeth hurried from the room. Her heart was sick and heavy from the terrible words that had flown between them. Up the stairs she went in a rustle of skirts and closed herself inside her room.

When she heard the slamming of the front door that meant he had gone, Elizabeth sank onto her bed and cried for half an hour. She thought of his words over and over without once understanding how the proud and arrogant man had come to love her as ardently as he proclaimed.

CHAPTER 6

LATER, Elizabeth returned to the parlor with her book though her head ached fiercely from crying and the tumult of her emotions.

Recalling Mr. Darcy's words of affection and loathing all in the space of one terribly offensive marriage proposal was confounding. While lying on her bed spent from her tears, the idea of a man like Mr. Darcy professing his love and desire to marry her had been terrifying and exciting all at once.

She could admit he was a most handsome gentleman. Elizabeth also knew she might have been happy to marry him had he not betrayed her sister. But the fact that he considered her beneath him in every manner assured there simply wasn't a way to bargain with her heart to reconsider her answer to his petition.

Still, something about the man excited her and had been the stuff of dreams that woke her in the night since his arrival in Kent.

As she paced the parlor thinking of his incredible confession and proposal and her subsequent refusal, Elizabeth heard the front door of the cottage open and Charlotte's happy greeting drift through the house.

Stepping through the parlor door, Elizabeth stopped and looked about for a sign of her cousin. "Charlotte, where is Mr. Collins? Did he not return with you?"

Charlotte smiled and took Elizabeth's hand. "He will be along shortly dear. How is your head? I wish I could have stayed behind with you. Lady Catherine was in rare form today and I am quite pleased to be home once more."

Elizabeth lifted her free hand to her forehead and enjoyed the coolness of her palm. The ache had worsened, of course, after Mr. Darcy's visit. "I fear it is no better. Perhaps I ought to lie down before dinner."

Taking her friend's hand, Charlotte opened the cottage door again and pulled Elizabeth along behind her. "The fresh air will do you good, Lizzy.

Come out and let us sit for a while before Mr. Collins returns."

Knowing her friend was right, Elizabeth stepped out and immediately drew in a deep breath. The air was cool and quite soothing against her heated skin and she felt a calm descend over her heart.

Kent was lovely and she was indeed happy she had made the trip to visit Charlotte. Meeting Anne de Bourgh had been another lovely turn of events though her mother was a terribly snobbish lady. It must be a family trait that skipped Miss Anne entirely.

Not thinking clearly, Elizabeth slipped and gave away the news of her visitor. "Tis such a lovely day, I ought to have taken a walk after Mr. Darcy left."

Charlotte turned and searched her friend's face. "Mr. Darcy came? While we were away?"

Elizabeth wished she could take back the comment but knew Charlotte would not rest until she had been given every detail. Instead of pacing, Elizabeth stood her ground. "Charlotte, you must not say a word to Mr. Collins. He would be most angry with me."

Charlotte shook her head. "Lizzy, you could not have known Mr. Darcy might come for a visit when we ourselves had no idea."

Elizabeth placed a hand on Charlotte's arm to interrupt. "It wasn't his visit, Charlotte, but the reason for it that will anger my cousin. Mr. Darcy proposed to me."

Charlotte was stunned into silence. Elizabeth lowered her gaze to the stones that made a path from the gate to the front door of the cottage.

After several long moments of silence, Charlotte patted Elizabeth's hand. "You must have accepted his proposal?"

"No, Charlotte, I did not! I sent him away. I told him I could never be prevailed upon to marry him." Elizabeth's words tumbled forth as she feared her courage might fail.

Elizabeth had never seen Charlotte lose her composure but in this instance her friend was incensed. "Have you lost all reason? I once thought you were the most intelligent, discerning person I knew but the Lizzy that stands before me now defies all logic. You have never been kind to Mr. Darcy, but this is beyond the pale."

Charlotte had dropped Elizabeth's hand before she began to speak and now she simply stood before her friend with her own hands in the air in disbelief.

Elizabeth hugged herself against the sharp sting of Charlotte's words. She had not expected her dearest friend to understand her refusal completely but a bit of sympathy at her plight would have been welcome. "Charlotte, how can you say such things? You know Mr. Darcy's sins. I have told you of his interference with Mr. Bingley and Jane and how he mistreated Mr. Wickham. How could you think I would consent to marry such a man?"

Not moved for a moment by Elizabeth's explanations, Charlotte did not spare her friend's feelings on the matter. "As you told me yourself, Jane has come to accept Mr. Bingley's fickle nature and with much grace considering the terrible position he put her in before our neighbors in Hertfordshire. There was gossip to be certain, but your sister rose above it. Yet you stand here with it burning in your heart as a mark against Mr. Darcy? If Mr. Bingley were any kind of gentleman with feelings for Jane, he would not have been persuaded to leave her side."

Elizabeth was shocked by Charlotte's words. Before she might defend herself, Charlotte continued scolding her dear friend. "As to the business with Mr. Wickham — he is a scoundrel and a rake, that one. Father told me of debts he ran up in Meryton that Mr. Darcy paid in spite of the rumors the man spread against his character. But, in your mind, Mr. Darcy is to blame for Mr. Wickham's misfortunes."

Elizabeth could not answer the charge Charlotte laid at her feet. She had not known her truest friend held such strong opinions about the matters concerning Mr. Bingley and Mr. Wickham, nor did she possess any knowledge of debts and repayment, and so she was not prepared to make a logical answer to Charlotte. Instead, she wondered how she might have been so mistaken about Mr. Darcy.

If all the world, including Jane and Charlotte, could see what she could not she did not deserve a man like Fitzwilliam Darcy.

Feeling tears threatening, Elizabeth was surprised as Charlotte's arms wrapped her in a gentle embrace. Allowing her tears to fall, she remained silent as Charlotte spoke again, this time softly.

"Oh Lizzy, you have been wrong about Mr. Darcy and now you must speak with him if only to offer an apology. He is a good man, one you deserve though you may think you do not. Come, let us go in before Mr. Collins finds us here on the doorstep behaving as foolish girls. On the morrow, I will go with you to Rosings to right this wrong."

CHAPTER 7

Fitzwilliam Darcy strode the length of the library at Rosings three times before his cousin, Colonel Richard Fitzwilliam, entered the room. The Colonel had traveled with him to Kent for Easter to pay a call to their aunt, Lady Catherine de Bourgh.

Lady Catherine was the elder sister of Mr. Darcy's mother, Lady Anne Darcy, whom he still missed a great deal though she had been dead many years hence. The only way one might have known the two grand ladies were sisters was to have known the Fitzwilliam family, for their dispositions were as night and day with Lady Catherine being the ill-tempered sister of the pair.

Richard crossed the room and poured himself a bit of brandy as he watched his cousin's agitated pacing. Fitzwilliam Darcy only did such when he was deep in thought and so Richard decided to take his drink and have a seat by the fireplace.

Rosings was a lovely estate in Kent, nearly as grand as Pemberley, but the spring weather bore more resemblance to late winter than he particularly liked for the season.

Allowing the spirits in his cup and the dancing flames of the fireplace to ease his memories of the chilly weather, Richard sighed as warmth enveloped his weary bones.

He'd been recently too long gone from England as a soldier in His Majesty's finest and his mother, Margaret Fitzwilliam, had been quite unwilling for him to make his customary trip to Kent this year with his cousin. Richard had keenly missed Darcy's unparalleled company and had promised his mother he would not stay a moment longer than necessary before returning to London.

Mr. Darcy ceased his infernal pacing just as Richard was about to rise and refill his glass. Instead, Darcy held out a hand for the crystal vessel and raised a brow. "Shall it be more brandy, then?"

Richard ran a hand through his hair and yawned deeply. "Indeed, Darcy, I require several such portions to relieve the chill in my bones. Riding about this countryside is comforting, likely the best part of visiting Kent in my opinion, but today the sun refuses to grace us with even a bit of warmth."

Mr. Darcy handed his glass back and instead retrieved the decanter and another glass before returning to settle comfortably beside his cousin.

Richard knew by Darcy's uncustomary action, the easy acceptance of an excuse to imbibe before the fire, that the man likely needed an ear to bend. He knew it must concern one Miss Elizabeth Bennet but held his tongue in order not to dissuade his cousin from divulging that which vexed him so greatly.

Miss Elizabeth Bennet was quite lovely and Richard had walked with her about the grounds of Rosings several times since arriving in Kent. Her conversation was lively and full of wit. Richard enjoyed her company immensely but knew Darcy held a deep admiration for the woman he could not hide.

This was not an unusual habit of his cousin, it was the way Darcy managed his own emotions before sharing them with those he trusted most, Richard being the chief recipient of Darcy's confidence. They were more like brothers than Richard and his own brother, James, but still Darcy was reticent to burden Richard with his struggles.

Fitzwilliam Darcy was the most eligible bachelor

of the Ton and as such, well, the man was hounded by mothers who thrust their daughters before him without remorse or regret.

After the two had sipped their brandy for a few moments in silence, Richard turned to his cousin. "Darcy, I know you are most decidedly troubled and that Miss Elizabeth is likely the cause. You may as well tell me now so that we might settle upon a course of action."

Darcy set his half empty glass upon the ornate table between them. He had hoped to recover from his visit to the parson's cottage where Miss Elizabeth had broken his heart without good reason or remorse a few hours prior. "I might have known you would see through my customary pacing to the truth of the matter. Be that as it may, I do not think you will believe what I have done and how terribly wrong I have been."

Richard finished his drink and stretched his long legs before motioning for Darcy to continue. "Have out with it, man. Aunt Catherine will soon be seeking to draw us into a gloomy evening in the parlor to discuss the details of spring planting and her boundless generosity to her poor tenants."

Mr. Darcy knew his cousin was correct. Lady Catherine repeated her oft told tales each and every spring for as long as he could remember and this year would be no different. She was the wisest, most benevolent, principled and proper peer of the realm and her subjects were wholly unaware, and therefore not properly grateful, of their distinct fortune in having her attention focused upon their daily lives.

A silly smile flitted across his lips for a moment before disappearing as quickly as it came. Had he not gone to pay a call on Miss Elizabeth, the humor brought on by his aunt's self-importance might have been more amusing.

He rested his elbows on his knees as he peered into the fire. "I foolishly offered a proposal of marriage to Miss Elizabeth and she soundly refused me. Can you imagine it? Any number of ladies with better connections and quite a larger dowry would have lied and schemed to have sat where she did this afternoon and swoon before my offer. But not Miss Elizabeth Bennet, oh no sir! My character was deemed abhorrent and my offer thoroughly rejected. I am the last man she might be prevailed upon to marry."

The library door was slightly ajar from Richard's earlier entrance and the slight, soft gasp on the other side of the thick door did not carry into the room. A shadow outside the library door trembled and Miss

Anne de Bourgh hurried to the entryway of Rosings after a moment's hesitation in which she knew she must go to the parsonage on her cousin's behalf.

Miss Elizabeth Bennet had become a delightful companion for the young mistress of Rosings in the weeks since her arrival. Anne de Bourgh could think of nothing more than rushing to her friend's side.

Knowing her mother would be angry did she know of her daughter's intentions, the slip of a young lady retrieved her spencer from a closet near the front door and ventured out without giving notice to anyone, not her maid nor even the butler.

Hurrying her steps, Anne de Bourgh walked briskly to the stables and had the groom ready her gig. He began to refuse her but Anne spoke sharply to the man. "Do you wish to face the wrath of my mother for denying me your services?"

The groom's face paled considerably at this outburst and he hastened to do the young miss's bidding. He knew either way her ladyship was likely to have his hide. In a trice, the groom had Anne's gig ready but managed another warning for his mistress. "Forgive me, Miss, but your mother will be most angry. Perhaps you ought to wait until she, or one of your cousins, might accompany you?"

Anne ignored the man and climbed easily into

the small gig. She'd driven it about Rosings and Hunsford many a time and had no concerns about doing so again under such circumstances, even though the groom was right to warn her to wait for her mother.

In this instance, she had no choice in the matter. Lady Catherine would send her to her rooms and certainly instruct the groom never to follow the young mistress's instructions again. She simply had to speak with Miss Elizabeth this night.

With a smart flick of her wrist, Anne de Bourgh was off in a mad dash to the parson's cottage. Though Anne knew little of the ways of courtship between a lady and a gentleman from having been lonely at Rosings for years without the benefit of balls, dances, or soirees, she knew well enough that her cousin Fitzwilliam was quite taken with Elizabeth Bennet.

The manner in which his eyes followed Miss Elizabeth as she crossed the room to play the piano forte of an evening was most romantic. His repressed feelings were the stuff of the novels Anne hid from her mother.

After a few minutes of driving her gig in the cool evening air, Anne began to shiver though she wore a heavy dress under her spencer. It was not often she was allowed to go out upon a spring day, let alone a spring evening, for her mother feared the air would kill her.

To distract herself from the chill that crept through the folds of her skirt, Anne imagined how lovely a summer wedding at Pemberley might be in the splendid gardens and a smile bloomed on her pretty face. Anne de Bourgh, had she been allowed a season, would have been as popular as her cousin Fitzwilliam Darcy. Though she was frail, her beauty was of a classical, timeless nature.

Her hair was golden and featured lustrous, loose waves that framed her heart-shaped face perfectly. Her light blue eyes were the exact shade of the corn-flower blooms along the side of the road and her smile made them brighter, infusing them with a warmth rarely seen in one so highly born and favored.

How she longed for a season but had given up hopes for such a dream over the years. Her mother had told her she was to marry her cousin and so there was no need for a season. But Fitzwilliam was like unto a brother in her mind. She could not conceive of a life married to him, nor of bearing him an heir, though she loved him a great deal.

Now that Miss Elizabeth was in Kent and Anne had seen with her own eyes the young lady's affect upon her handsome, bachelor cousin, perhaps her chance to go to London for a season was within her grasp? Her mother could not compel Fitzwilliam to marry her, for she had overheard their arguments each spring for several years on the matter. She and Fitzwilliam dearly loved one another but not in a romantic fashion.

Knowing that she would soon be at the cottage, Anne did not fear the shadows of the evening that lengthened across the tree-lined lane. She would implore Miss Elizabeth to accompany her to Rosings and sort out the misunderstanding and there would be a lovely wedding.

Flicking the reins once more, Anne de Bourgh bounced on her seat as the horse cantered down the familiar lane.

CHAPTER 8

The gig driven by Anne de Bourgh arrived at the parson's cottage as Elizabeth and Charlotte stood in the doorway. They glanced at one another with worry plainly written in the crease of a brow for one and the bite of a bottom lip for the other.

Though it was late and the visit unusual, the pair hurried to the gate wondering why the young mistress of Rosings had come.

"Miss de Bourgh," Charlotte began as she moved closer to the cottage gate, "what has happened to bring you to our home so late?"

Anne smiled at Mrs. Collins and shrugged her shoulders. There was no way she might know whether Miss Elizabeth had spoken of her cousin's proposal to Mrs. Collins and so she spoke as though she had no knowledge of the matter. "I wished to take a bit of air, Mrs. Collins, and I thought I might stop and visit for a time."

Mr. Collins came around the side of the cottage at the noise of Anne's arrival and glanced about as though Lady Catherine might be lurking nearby. "I say, Miss Anne, where is your mother?"

Anne had not intended to draw the attention of the parson but she ought to have known he would be home at this hour. "Mr. Collins, mother is at home with my cousins. I only stopped upon seeing Mrs. Collins and Miss Elizabeth by the door."

The parson gave a worried smile and glanced to his wife before turning to address Miss de Bourgh once more. "Would you like for me to see you back to Rosings? It is getting late."

"I would not impose sir, but I would speak with Miss Elizabeth for a time if I may."

Knowing he could not refuse the daughter of his patroness any request she might make of him, Mr. Collins turned and looked at his cousin Elizabeth. Certainly she would be happy to see Miss de Bourgh safely home. "Go on then, Cousin Elizabeth, see her home. Lady Catherine shall be worried. 'Tis a small favor as you are quite happy to walk about the grounds at all hours."

Elizabeth ignored her cousin's disdain for her

beloved habit of roaming the countryside and went to lift the latch on the gate.

Miss de Bourgh was unable to conceal her joy as Elizabeth climbed easily into the handsome gig. "Miss Elizabeth, I would speak with you alone. I will not rest until you have heard all that I must say."

Elizabeth wondered what the young mistress of Rosings was about but since they had become friends, she was happy to ride back to Rosings and entertain conversation

Turning to wave to her family still standing in the cottage yard, Elizabeth called out as Miss Anne sent the horse on its way, "I shall not be long!"

Once the visitor from Rosings was certain they were out of earshot of the parson and his wife, the young lady began her entreaty. "Miss Elizabeth, I overheard the news that my cousin proposed to you earlier today and I came to persuade you to reconsider your answer."

Elizabeth had not thought for a moment that Miss de Bourgh might know of Mr. Darcy's visit and certainly not of his proposal. Her cheeks burned with embarrassment at her current situation. "How did you hear such a thing?"

Anne let the horse set the pace and turned to stare at her friend. "Fitzwilliam did not announce it to the house if that is where your concern lies. Yet, I overheard his conversation with Richard in the library."

Elizabeth gasped and covered her mouth in astonishment. While she knew Miss Anne would not betray her cousin's trust willingly, the worst possible outcome was Lady Catherine de Bourgh finding her daughter was out in the darkness of evening without a proper escort and the reason for such a jaunt. "You must return home now. Your mother will be quite angry you have come looking for me alone in the dark."

Though she was thoroughly shocked by the turn of events and knew for certain Mr. Darcy would be mortified by Miss Anne's actions, Elizabeth would not speak of his proposal. If Anne de Bourgh had risked her mother's wrath only to intervene on her cousin's behalf, the poor girl was quite mistaken to think her actions could right Elizabeth's mistake.

"Listen to me, there is no time to waste. You must tell me why you have refused my cousin so that we may settle this thing tonight."

Elizabeth could not believe her ears. Miss Anne de Bourgh wished to repair the damage she had done. "I cannot possibly face Mr. Darcy this night. What would your mother think of such a visit?

Though I admit I was wrong, I do not think Mr. Darcy meant for you to know of our meeting."

The young mistress of Rosings knew they were approaching the house and she must persuade her friend. "It is too late now. Whatever my cousin hoped before, his voice as he spoke of your refusal broke my heart Miss Elizabeth. Would you leave him alone to think you do not care for him? If you do love him and have changed your mind, come with me."

Elizabeth would not and shook her head vigorously. "This will not do. If your mother finds that you have been out to bring me back to Rosings, I fear her wrath. I shall come in the morning to speak with Mr. Darcy, I promise."

Anne was not happy with Elizabeth's decision but she had done her best to help her beloved cousin and his lady love. "I will distract Mother tomorrow so that you might see Fitzwilliam without her interference."

Elizabeth began to refuse Anne's offer of assistance when a dark shadow streaked across the road in front of the gig. In a moment the horse spooked and reared up on its hind legs causing the gig to pitch to one side.

The screams of the young mistress frightened the horse further and Anne de Bourgh was thrown clear of the conveyance as Elizabeth grabbed at her shoulders. Scrabbling for purchase inside the gig, Elizabeth cried out as her elbow banged against a metal rail.

Letting go and cradling her arm, Elizabeth was tossed to the floor of the gig as the horse bucked again. She was thrown backwards and slid helplessly across the floor and out into the road.

Having the presence of mind to roll away from the rocking, swaying gig, Elizabeth stumbled to her feet and searched the ground for Anne de Bourgh. The poor girl was perilously close to the gig and lying still as a stone.

Her mind no longer anchored in reality, Elizabeth screamed and lunged towards her friend. With Anne in her arms, she trembled as the wheels crashed behind them. Covering Anne's body with her own, Elizabeth cried out and prayed for their deliverance. A wheel broke and that side of the gig crashed to the ground as the horse took off in a gallop.

Elizabeth felt something heavy strike her head and she collapsed in a heap beside the limp body of Anne de Bourgh.

Mr. Darcy quit the library with Richard and thought to retire to his rooms before they might be drawn into the parlor with his Aunt Catherine.

After his failure to secure Miss Elizabeth's hand at the parson's cottage, Darcy was in no mood to endure the company of his aunt.

His plans were interrupted by the strident voice of his aunt in the entryway as he approached the stairs. Mr. Darcy saw that a groom from the stables stood just inside the front door. The man's head was hung low as Lady Catherine cut him to the quick.

"How have you allowed my daughter to leave in her gig so late in the evening without sending word to me? Where has she gone?"

Mr. Darcy and the Colonel rushed to stand beside Lady Catherine and waited for the terrified man to speak. "I do not know where she has gone, your ladyship, only that she has not returned. I could not rest knowing she is out alone."

Lady Catherine ordered the butler to send riders out to look for her daughter. Instead, Mr. Darcy sent the groom to ready horses for himself and Richard. "Make haste man, my aunt will likely see you sacked but I may speak on your behalf for coming to tell us of Anne's absence instead of going home to your bed."

The groom was off in a trice eager to please his employer's nephew. There was little reason to believe he would have a job come the morning, but there was nothing to be lost by helping recover the young mistress of Rosings.

"Aunt Catherine, it is likely she has simply taken a turn about the property and shall come home while we are out searching. Come Richard, let us be off before we lose what little light is left in the sky."

Mr. Darcy lingered before his aunt as he thought to assure her they would find Anne, but she waved him on his way. He turned smartly on his heel and disappeared into the darkening evening.

Richard followed, catching up quickly. "Darcy, what purpose would Anne have for going out alone this time of evening? Do you think she might have overheard our conversation in the library? She is good friends with Miss Elizabeth."

Darcy had not thought of it, for Anne was most usually in the parlor or her rooms. "I'd be surprised to hear it, Richard. You know as well as I she spends a great deal of time in her rooms."

Richard gave a nervous chuckle. "Indeed! Aunt

Catherine is forever sending the poor girl upstairs at the least provocation. Still, I had no idea Anne was allowed out in her gig alone."

Mr. Darcy took the reins the groom offered and quickly mounted his horse. "I daresay Anne slips her mother's watchful eye from time to time and Aunt Catherine is none the wiser for the most part. In any case, let us split up and search."

The groom took a third horse and mounted without delay. "I would search with you sir, for I ought not to have allowed the young mistress to leave alone."

Darcy nodded his agreement, pleased that the servant was attempting to make amends for his error in judgment.

Richard mounted his horse and followed Darcy and the groom to the gravel drive in front of Rosings. "Shall I go the way that leads to the parson's cottage? I could stop and ask whether they've seen Anne."

Mr. Darcy nodded. He had no desire to meet with Elizabeth Bennet for a second time in the space of a few hours. "That would be wise, I think. I shall ride out towards Hunsford in case she has gone that way. Take the groom with you and we shall meet here again hopefully with Anne in tow."

The men parted ways and Mr. Darcy was

pleased to leave Rosings behind. His day had been an abysmal failure and he longed to be up with the sunrise and leave for London with or without Richard by his side. He would spend the remainder of his holiday at his townhouse with his sister and the Matlocks. Come the summer, they would all leave Town for Pemberley.

Miss Elizabeth's refusal still stung deeply though he had told himself at least a hundred times that she did not truly know his character. If she did, she would have understood what his poor choice of words meant instead of how they sounded.

He had been nothing less than a gentleman his entire life. It was not a fault of his that she could not see the truth of her connections. As to Wickham, well, there was nothing he might say on that score as the truth would incriminate his dear sister.

Still, his mind could not escape the knowledge of his heart. He loved Elizabeth Bennet with a surety that would not be denied. The idea of leaving Kent without having secured her hand sent his heart plummeting to his stomach. Fitzwilliam Darcy was not accustomed to losing but in this affair of the heart, he had been bested and found he cared not for the feeling.

Mr. Darcy nudged his horse into a trot as he

came upon the town of Hunsford. The streets were empty and the shoppes closed for the day. He stopped his horse at a corner and listened for the sound of any other that might be passing through.

He was greeted by silence for the most part. Only the clanging of a bell in the distance, and the sharp bark of a dog nearby, punctuated the evening air. Turning his horse back towards Rosings, Mr. Darcy hoped Richard had been more successful in his search.

CHAPTER 9

Colonel Fitzwilliam rode with careful deliberation down the dark lane with the groom following behind. He swept the area with a penetrating gaze in search of his cousin's gig. He tried not to worry but it was not in Anne's nature to be out alone after dark.

He knew for certain that even if she had fallen into the habit of sneaking out to drive her gig from time to time, she would not have done so late into the evening without escort.

Truly, there was little to fear as every tenant and servant of Rosings and inhabitant of Hunsford knew who the young mistress was and would not see her come to harm could they prevent such a circumstance.

No, Richard was not concerned for her safety. He was more concerned that his cousin, in her delicate health, would fall ill due to the chill in the night air.

As he hurried his pace down the lane towards the parson's cottage, he thought of Darcy's failed proposal and Miss Elizabeth. He knew their visit to Rosings was now near its end and though he regretted it, he would leave with Darcy.

Before he might consider their departure further, a horse met him in the lane pulling the remnants of a broken gig. Richard turned and shouted to the groom. "Catch him and see that he is returned to Rosings. I fear something terrible has happened to Miss Anne. Send a wagon back this way with several men."

The groom hurried to do Richard's bidding as the Colonel nudged his horse into action. The animal was spooked by the behavior of the runaway horse but Richard skillfully settled the beast's nerves.

Turning a bend in the road, he saw two figures lying on the ground. Swiftly dropping from his horse, Richard ran to the unfortunate pair only to find one was indeed his cousin and the other Miss Elizabeth Bennet.

Not knowing whether he ought to move them before the groom returned with a wagon from Rosings, Richard covered Miss Elizabeth with his greatcoat and turned to examine Anne as best he could.

Serving in His Majesty's finest had left him with useful knowledge of injuries in the field as he had helped care for the men under his command, though such was not his habit nor specialty.

Carefully searching his cousin's limbs for injury, Richard was satisfied there were none to be found. He sent up a silent prayer of thanks and tenderly pulled Anne into his arms to warm her body. Her head fell against his chest and the Colonel hoped there were no hidden injuries he might worsen in his attempt to shield her from the night air.

He dared not touch Miss Elizabeth as she lay awkwardly prone upon the ground. At least his coat provided some comfort to the poor young woman.

As he sat waiting for the men from Rosings, Richard wondered how Miss Elizabeth had come to be here with his cousin. He knew the ladies had become good friends during the holiday but could not think of a reason for Anne to have gone to the parsonage.

The idea that perhaps Anne had overhead his conversation with Darcy in the library entered his head for a second time that evening and he hoped he was wrong. His Aunt Catherine would blame Darcy and Miss Elizabeth for Anne's terrible circumstances if that were the cause of his cousin's absence from Rosings.

Richard glanced at Anne's face as another silent prayer left his lips and her eyelashes fluttered open. Her beautiful face was paler than usual and Richard held himself perfectly still though he longed to hug her tightly.

A moan escaped her lips and Richard fought back tears. "Shhhh, my dear, I am here and the horse has gone. I shall have you home as soon as the men come with the wagon."

He smoothed the damp hair from her brow and touched her cheek gently. Her eyes grew rounder and she tried to move but Richard would not allow it. "You must remain still, poppet. You are most certainly injured and it will serve no good purpose for you to move about."

Anne ceased her struggle and buried her face in Richard's chest. Gently, he tightened his hold on the frail young woman and laid his cheek against her head. He thought to ask her about Miss Elizabeth but decided there was no pressing need for that information. There would be time later to sort out the truth of the matter.

He looked up as the sound of a wagon trundling

down the lane reached his ears. Blessed saints, the men had come!

When they arrived, he directed them to place Miss Elizabeth in the bed of the wagon first and then he stood and was helped into the wagon with Anne still in his arms.

'Twas a most uncomfortable ride back to Rosings and Richard feared the young ladies might be injured further before they arrived. "Slow down, man!" he yelled to the driver, "Tis injured ladies here and not pigs to the market."

The driver slowed the horses and Richard turned to the groom who rode alongside the wagon. "Have you spoken with my aunt or seen Darcy since last we met?"

The man shook his head. "Aye, sir, I did tell her ladyship that we suspect Miss Anne is hurt. I have not seen Mr. Darcy since we parted at Rosings earlier."

At this news, Richard relaxed his hold on his cousin but kept her within his embrace.

As the wagon approached the drive in front of Rosings, Richard saw Darcy standing with their aunt. Many of the house servants were assembled behind them holding up lanterns against the darkness.

It was a welcome sight and the battle hardened military man felt a weight lift from his shoulders. Soon the two injured ladies would be safe and warm inside the house. Thinking suddenly of the parson, he turned to the groom who still rode beside the wagon. "Go and tell Mr. and Mrs. Collins what has happened. I daresay they are terribly worried for Miss Elizabeth."

The man turned his horse and dashed back the way the wagon had come. Richard was angry with himself for not thinking of it before but at least the ladies had been found.

Mr. Darcy hurried to the wagon with the intention of taking Anne from his cousin but stopped when Richard shook his head. "You might wish to see to Miss Elizabeth, Darcy. She was lying in the road beside Anne."

His face a study in confusion at his cousin's words, Darcy peered into the bed of the wagon and flinched when he saw Miss Elizabeth was indeed injured. "How did she come to be in that gig with Anne?"

Richard braced his hand against the side of the wagon and slid across the rough planks as best he could while keeping Anne sheltered with his other arm. She'd grown quiet during the ride to Rosings and he feared she had fainted once more.

Resting his free hand on his cousin's broad shoulder, Richard stepped down from the wagon and clutched Anne's small body tightly to his frame. His voice trembled as his frail cousin moaned in pain. "I have no answer for that Darcy, only that I found them together lying upon the road."

Watching helplessly as Richard carried Anne up the stone steps of Rosings with a terribly shaken Lady Catherine by his side, Mr. Darcy turned to the bed of the wagon as the men from the stables began to remove Elizabeth Bennet's still form.

To one of the footmen, he gave an order. "You must go to London, to Darcy House and have my butler send for Dr. Green to come to us. He is my personal physician and will know what must be done."

The footman made haste to do his bidding. Mr. Darcy waved away the men who were attempting to remove Miss Elizabeth from the wagon and took her into his arms, biting back the tears that threatened in the quiet darkness of the evening. Mr. Darcy followed in Richard's footsteps attempting to avoid the concerned stares of the household staff.

Once inside, he waited as a maid came to him.

"Will you bring her upstairs, sir? I can ready the room next to Miss Anne."

Mr. Darcy nodded but was startled when the voice of his aunt thundered against his agreement with the maid. "She shall not stay here. See that she is taken to the parson's cottage. My Anne was obviously led to treachery by the foolish chit."

Ignoring his aunt's directive, Mr. Darcy moved past Lady Catherine and started up the stairs holding tightly to Elizabeth Bennet. He would not release her until they were upstairs and the room the maid had indicated was made ready.

Lady Catherine flew to his side and pulled on Elizabeth's limp arm. "Did you hear me, Fitzwilliam? She shall not stay here!"

Mr. Darcy turned his back on his aunt to block her from touching Miss Elizabeth again. His voice held the threat of his iron will as he rebuked her order. "She will remain at Rosings until she is well, Aunt Catherine. I have sent for my physician from London. He shall tend them both when he arrives. Go to your daughter for pity's sake. The poor girl needs you now more than ever."

He continued his steady pace up the stairs with the frightened maid going before him. Instead of remaining silent, Mr. Darcy assured the young servant girl all would be well. "My aunt is not herself at the moment and you must listen to me. I promise you shall have your job if you do as I say. Now, go ready that room for Miss Elizabeth."

The maid glanced over her shoulder at her employer but soon turned and hurried on her way when the mistress of Rosings followed them up the stairs.

Lady Catherine passed Mr. Darcy and gave a disgusted noise as she assured him she was not pleased with his disobedience. "When she is well, she must leave here without delay. I will not abide her presence a moment longer."

Mr. Darcy did not reply to his aunt, for his beloved was injured and in dire need of the best of care and he would see to it that she wanted for nothing. Besides, his aunt had placed blame upon the poor lady without a shred of proof and arguing with her when it would solve nothing seemed beneath him.

Entering the drafty room behind the maid, he waited patiently as the young servant rushed about the room lighting a fire and turning back the counterpane of the elegant four poster bed. "Sir, shall I sit with her while we wait for the apothecary? Her ladyship sent for him as soon as she heard the news of Miss Anne's accident."

Mr. Darcy almost refused the offer but instead nodded his approval. "Yes please, if she stirs you must come for me. I shall only be in my cousin's rooms."

He would return to Miss Elizabeth's side regardless of her state after he visited his injured cousin.

As Mr. Darcy entered Anne's bedroom, Lady Catherine paced about as the maid checked the fire and pulled the drapes closed. Mr. Darcy nodded to the young servant as a means of dismissal and waited until the door closed to speak with his aunt.

"Aunt Catherine, come sit with me and let us think of what must be done. I know you have sent for the apothecary but I have a rider dispatched to London for my physician. Is there more I might do?"

Lady Catherine crossed her arms and stared imperiously at her nephew. "Do you know why Anne might have taken off in her gig at such a late hour? And how on earth she came to be in the company of Miss Elizabeth Bennet? Unless you are able to explain those mysteries to my satisfaction, there is little you might do to be of assistance."

Mr. Darcy had no idea why Miss Elizabeth and Anne were together other than the remark Richard had made earlier, when they had gone to search for Anne.

Not knowing for certain whether Richard's conjecture was the truth, he dared not make mention of it to his aunt. She already believed Miss Elizabeth to be responsible for Anne's condition and the secret of his proposal would only inflame her suspicions. There was nothing to be gained by guessing what might have sent Anne off in her gig. As soon as either young lady was recovered, they could seek the answers to those questions.

"Aunt Catherine, I have no idea what prompted my cousin to fancy an evening jaunt. I only hope that she and Miss Elizabeth shall soon be restored."

CHAPTER 10

ON THE NEXT AFTERNOON, when the physician from London had seen both young ladies, Mr. Darcy stood in the upstairs hallway with Lady Catherine and Mr. and Mrs. Collins as the man gave his impression of the situation.

"I do not believe either young lady suffers grave internal injuries, though you must not think them entirely well just yet because of my opinion. Miss Anne seems fine other than a vague recollection of all that transpired in the accident. There is some bruising on her left side that will make it difficult for her to sit up for long periods of time. Miss Elizabeth, on the other hand, suffered a blow to the head and will take some time to heal completely. I am most concerned for her as she has not yet awakened."

Lady Catherine could not conceal her exasperation. "Is that all you have to say on the matter? Darcy has sent to London for the best physician and this is all I am to expect?"

Mr. Darcy moved closer to his aunt and placed his hand on her arm to calm her, for she had been by Anne's side since Richard had brought her home the evening before. "The doctor has given his prognosis and there is nothing we might do now but follow his advice to the letter."

Turning his attention to the physician, Mr. Darcy kept his voice low in order to encourage his aunt to mimic his own composure. "Dr. Green, we shall follow your recommendations but I hoped you might be able to stay a fortnight so that we might be confident in our care of the ladies. They are both so dear to our families."

Lady Catherine gasped and meant to deliver a set down to her nephew for daring to pretend Elizabeth Bennet mattered in the least to her family, but Mr. Darcy turned to Mr. and Mrs. Collins. "Miss Elizabeth shall remain at Rosings. There are many servants available to assist with her care. Mrs. Collins, shall I write to the Bennet family or would you prefer to deliver the news?"

Charlotte looked to her husband before answering. "I think we ought to write to Jane in London so that she might come and help care for Lizzy. A separate letter can be sent to Longbourn."

Mr. Collins glanced warily at his patroness who had gone dangerously quiet. The woman was certainly not herself but he felt he must register his disagreement with Mr. Darcy's plans. "Cousin Elizabeth should recover at the cottage as well as she might here at Rosings. Though we are humbled by your consideration, Mr. Darcy, I would hate to impose upon the kindness of Lady Catherine."

The physician spoke up before the mistress of Rosings might reply. "Sir, it is my strongest recommendation that your cousin remain here until she is recovered. Moving her about now is quite ill advised. Unless there is a compelling reason why she must leave, I register my strongest objections. I shall remain in Kent for the fortnight Mr. Darcy has requested. With the ladies situated together under one roof my efforts will be greatly enhanced."

Mr. Darcy was pleased by the physician's adamant words that settled the recovery of Miss Elizabeth at Rosings. "Let us call for the maids who shall attend our young ladies. They must sit with Dr. Green and take his advice on what must be done. Shall we adjourn to the parlor?"

Lady Catherine glanced worriedly toward

Anne's door. Her anger had been smothered by her nephew's skillful handling of the situation. "I would not leave Anne for longer than necessary. If the maids are to come with us to the parlor, who will sit with her? She is sleeping now but I do worry."

Charlotte stepped forward and spoke kindly to her husband's patroness. Lady Catherine was not her favorite by any means but Charlotte's heart was touched by the woman's concern for her only child. "I shall sit with Anne and look in on Lizzy. Surely all will be well for an hour?"

Mr. Collins puffed out his chest with pride at his wife's thoughtfulness. To him, it was indicative of his talent as a good husband rather than the innate kindness of his wife.

Lady Catherine seemed to waver in her devotion for a moment. Charlotte seized the opportunity. "I promise if she should flutter so much as a lash, I will come for you myself."

Mr. Darcy thanked Mrs. Collins for her kindness and offered his arm to his aunt. "Come, Aunt Catherine, we must learn what is to be done for our Anne and Miss Elizabeth. The sooner we get on with the task, the sooner you may return to your daughter's side."

The party left Charlotte alone in the hallway

and she quietly entered the young mistress of Rosing's rooms. As she straightened the covers on the bed, she found a book.

Turning the book over, the parson's wife gasped at the title. It was a racy novel of the sort many young ladies read but seldom allowed others to see. Smiling, she flipped through the pages and read silently. "Oh, Miss Anne, you are a romantic at heart. One who wishes for a dashing young gentleman, perhaps a viscount, to take you away from your lovely prison."

Charlotte replaced the novel beneath the covers where she'd found it, for she knew the young mistress would not wish for her mother to find it, and took Miss de Bourgh's hand gently in her own. "Well, you must get better for there is little chance your mother might allow your prince to enter this bedchamber."

A twinge of pity fell on Charlotte's heart for the lovely young woman and she bowed her head in prayer. Asking nothing for herself, she petitioned her heavenly Father on behalf of the blameless lass before her.

Moments later, Charlotte rose and quickly made her way to Elizabeth's room. The sight of her dearest friend pale and lying so very still upon the bed frightened Charlotte. "Oh Lizzy, what shall I tell Jane? And your parents?"

Taking Elizabeth's hand, she repeated her prayers again, this time for the friend she loved as a sister.

Reluctantly, Charlotte stood and placed a kiss on Elizabeth's forehead. "Once Miss Anne's maid has returned, I shall come sit with you and write a letter to Jane. She will come, Lizzy, and together we will see that you are well."

ঔ৺৩

JANE BENNET WAS STARTLED by the appearance of her aunt in the parlor door so that she dropped her embroidery. The woman's face was so pale that Jane worried she might faint. Rising quickly to her feet, she hurried to Madeline Gardiner's side. "What has happened?"

The woman held out a letter, her hand shaking terribly. "'Tis an express from Rosings, Elizabeth has been hurt. Charlotte says you must come as soon as you might."

Jane took the paper and read it quickly, making certain her aunt had gotten the terrible news right.

"Charlotte says there was an accident and Elizabeth and Miss de Bourgh were injured. How could such a thing happen?"

Aunt Madeline shook her head. "I do not know but you must leave today, Jane, and see to your sister. Charlotte is a good friend but if something happens to Lizzy," here she stopped and swiped at tears, "well, she should not be without family."

Jane did not bother to remind her aunt that Mr. Collins was family for she herself knew the woman meant family that loved her sister. "I shall go now and prepare a small trunk. Do you think Uncle will mind if I take a maid along on the post chaise to Kent?"

Madeline Gardiner shook her head. "He would not, though I wish I could go with you. In this state," she said and indicated her increasing middle, "Edward would not let me go along."

Just then, the butler came to them in the parlor with another express. "From the Matlock family, madam."

Aunt Madeline took the letter and shook her head. "Tis much to bear in one day. I wonder what they might need? They are related to Mr. Darcy if I am not mistaken. They hold a large estate to the north of Pemberley in Derbyshire."

Jane held out her hand and took the letter while guiding her aunt to her usual seat by the window. Worried for the woman, Jane called for a maid to bring tea. Retrieving the blue feathered fan her Uncle Gardiner had sent home with her rose silk that day she and Elizabeth had visited his warehouse, Jane placed it in her aunt's hand. "Here Aunt Madeline, fan yourself before you faint dead away."

As Jane read, Madeline Gardiner made use of the fan knowing her niece was right to be concerned. Though the spring had been cool in Town, the news of Elizabeth's injury had caused much distress and the room felt entirely too warm.

"Lady Matlock is in Town and says that she and Miss Darcy shall travel to Kent with her eldest son and offers that I might go with them. Mr. Darcy apparently advised them I might need to travel with them to Kent. They are to leave in a few hours," Jane refolded the missive and called for the butler.

She moved quickly to the writing desk by the window and dashed off a note accepting their offer. The butler stood by and eagerly took the missive when Jane was certain the ink had dried. "See that the Matlocks receive it within the half hour, please, and ready the carriage to take me there."

Aunt Madeline watched her butler hurry from the room and gave a sigh of relief. "What quick thinking, Jane! Forgive me, for I ought to have handled the particulars allowing you to go upstairs and arrange a trunk."

Jane took her aunt's hand and placed it against her cheek. The woman's skin had cooled and her color was returning. "You will sit right here and have tea while I see to that trunk. I won't be long, unless you need me to stay with you."

Madeline Gardiner shook her head. "I am better now, my dearest Janie, thank you. We must concentrate on getting you to Kent my dear. I shall be fine here in my own parlor."

Leaving her aunt in the capable hands of a young maid, Jane quit the parlor and hurried upstairs to prepare for her unplanned trip.

Her dearest sister lay injured at Rosings under the roof of a woman not likely to wish for such an imposition with her own daughter likewise afflicted. How had Elizabeth come to be in an accident with Miss Anne de Bourgh?

Shaking her head to push her thoughts aside, Jane moved about her room in the Gardiner townhouse without delay to ready her trunk. She was nervous to meet the Matlocks under such circumstances, and the sister of Mr. Darcy, but their offer was not one she could refuse.

Uncle Gardiner would rest easier to have her traveling in the company of such a family than taking a post chaise with just a young maid as a companion. Besides, her aunt was in much greater need of her small staff than Jane was at the moment.

Once she was prepared for her trip, Jane Bennet hurried downstairs. She left her Aunt Madeline at the door with a gentle embrace and hastened to board the Gardiner carriage to make her way to Matlock House in Grosvenor.

CHAPTER 11

MR. DARCY SAT in the hallway between the two rooms that held his cousin and his beloved. There had been little change in the few days since the accident and his Aunt Catherine remained at her daughter's bedside.

Could he think of any good in the terrible event, it was that the proud and haughty woman became devoted to her daughter.

Waiting was his least favorite pastime but Mr. Darcy would not leave his post for very long. The butler had come to find him an hour earlier and brought an express from London. His sister Georgiana and their favorite aunt, Margaret Fitzwilliam, would soon arrive. He hoped their presence might serve to distract Lady Catherine from running off the maids that cared for her daughter and Miss Elizabeth.

The maids much preferred to sit with Miss Elizabeth rather than deal with his Aunt Catherine's demands. He'd attempted to speak with her about it but she was as intractable as ever in her moods.

Dr. Green appeared in the hallway and Mr. Darcy stood to greet the man. "Doctor, I trust you slept well. If there is anything you require while at Rosings, I shall personally see it is done. I am pleased you were able to stay with us for a time."

Dr. Green nodded to Mr. Darcy. "Every consideration has been made on my behalf and I am most grateful, sir. Has there been any change in either lady's condition?"

Mr. Darcy shook his head sadly. "Not as yet, though the maids did say each seemed to suffer in the night."

The physician was thoughtful as he began to pace the hallway between the two rooms. "I must try something to awaken Miss Elizabeth today. I fear if she does not improve we may have her taken to London."

Mr. Darcy became concerned at this news. He knew the fact that his beloved had not awakened worried Dr. Green but now he became restless in his ability to do nothing that might be of help to his beloved.

Taking some sort of action appealed to him in a way sitting idly by did not. "Let us go in and see Miss Elizabeth. What have you in mind to awaken her, Green?"

The physician entered the room ahead of Mr. Darcy and spoke in a hushed tone. "I brought smelling salts I've mixed myself as most apothecaries do not prepare them as strongly as I prefer. It cannot make things worse but if it does not work, I would insist we arrange for the young lady to be taken to Town immediately."

Mr. Darcy understood the man's concern. Mr. Collins was not at Rosings to give the doctor his blessing so Mr. Darcy gave his as he moved to stand at Elizabeth's bedside. "Go ahead, Green, let us see if Miss Elizabeth reacts to the smelling salts."

The physician nodded and searched among the bottles he'd left on the bedside table the day before. "Here we are. Ammonium carbonate. As I said, 'tis quite a strong mixture. Let us see if it has any effect on our young lady."

Removing the stopper from the glass bottle, the physician took out his handkerchief and blotted the cloth with the strong liquid. Darcy caught a whiff from where he stood and wrinkled his nose. If such a strong odor did not awaken Miss Elizabeth he would send for his carriage to be made ready to carry her to London.

Dr. Green sat on the bed and waved the handkerchief before Miss Elizabeth's face. In a few moments, she came awake sputtering and covering her nose. After a bout of coughing, her voice trembled as she spoke. "What on earth? Where am I?"

Her eyes darted from Mr. Darcy to Dr. Green and her face crumpled in confusion. Tears flooded her eyes from the pain that enveloped her head. Elizabeth lifted both hands to her forehead and whimpered causing Mr. Darcy to take a seat beside her on the bed. "Miss Elizabeth, you are safe here at Rosings. There was an accident."

Dr. Green glanced at Mr. Darcy and shook his head. Quietly, he spoke to halt the man's speech. "We must not tax her with too many facts just this moment. Her head likely feels as though someone is inside pounding a hammer. Asking too much too soon will only make it worse."

Elizabeth covered her face and cried quietly as the physician stood and prepared a concoction from the other bottles he'd left on her table. "Darcy, send for a maid to bring up a pot of tea so I might dose her before the pain becomes too terrible for her to bear."

Mr. Darcy jumped to his feet and hurried into the hallway. One of the maids stepped out of Anne's rooms and he sent her for the tea. "Miss Elizabeth is awake! Hurry, we must see that she takes the medicine Dr. Green has prepared."

The maid gave a pleased smile at the news and clapped her hands. "Thank heavens! Miss Anne has been asking for her all through the day."

Mr. Darcy smiled at the sincere young woman and waved her on her way and returned to Miss Elizabeth's rooms.

Dr. Green was speaking softly to her and the poor lady's face went from dismay to outright frustration in the space of a moment. He must be telling her of the accident. Mr. Darcy wanted to comfort her but could not without causing more distress as he was uncertain of her feelings for him.

Instead he slipped back into the hallway and decided to give his cousin the news that her friend had awakened. He must allow Dr. Green to tend his beloved without interference.

When he entered Anne's bedroom, Lady Catherine sat beside her sleeping daughter and whispered a memory of her childhood days. Mr. Darcy was surprised at this display of tenderness and hated to interrupt. He cleared his throat and went to stand behind his aunt.

She turned at the noise he made and stood, dropping Anne's hand gently onto the counterpane. "Have you come to sit with us, Darcy? I would hope so since you have given so much of your time to that country chit next door."

Mr. Darcy ignored the barb and smiled at her, so happy was he that his Elizabeth had awakened. "I would sit with Anne as well, but you are ever by her side and I would not intrude."

Lady Catherine wondered what her nephew was about but as it was a relief to stand and move about the room, she simply listened as he continued speaking.

"Would you come into the hall with me? There is some news you may not have heard."

"But who will stay with Anne? I sent her maid away. How have I never known she was the most incompetent servant in this house? I would send her packing if Anne did not prefer her."

Mr. Darcy offered his arm. "We shall only be in the hallway for a moment. We can leave the doors open so that you might hear if she awakens and calls out."

The mistress of Rosings was tired, terribly so, and so she took her nephew's arm. "Only for a moment, Fitzwilliam. What news has come to Rosings?"

In the hallway, Dr. Green met them as he left Miss Elizabeth's room. He thought to give Lady Catherine the good news of her guest's improvement but the woman sent him to sit with her daughter. "Dr. Green, my nephew feels there is news I must know. Would you sit with Anne for a moment? She is sleeping now but earlier she was asking about that night. It seems she cannot recall the reason she was out in her gig. Is that to be expected even now?"

Dr. Green nodded. "Indeed. We must not press her. I suspect she is choosing not to recall the event in detail as it was surely most frightening."

The physician stepped away as Mr. Darcy informed his aunt that his sister and Lady Matlock would soon arrive. He suspected Miss de Bourgh would be more likely to confide her memories of the accident to Miss Darcy.

As Harry Green stood over Anne de Bourgh's sleeping form, he admired the beautiful, young mistress. He was not a rake nor a scoundrel, but the idea of holding Miss de Bourgh in his arms flitted through his mind.

Scolding himself for these most scandalous thoughts, Dr. Green took the seat Lady Catherine had left moments ago. Anne de Bourgh's eyelashes fluttered open and a look of terror filled her eyes as she saw her mother had gone.

Dr. Green was stricken to his heart at her expression. "Miss de Bourgh, it is only me, Dr. Green. Do you remember? I shall send for your mother now, please do not be afraid."

Anne breathed deeply and gave a whimper as pain pierced her left side. She reached for the doctor's hand and held on until it passed. "I am sorry, doctor. I did not recall who you were for a moment. I know now and I am pleased you are here with me."

He was most kind, his eyes full of concern and regret. Anne quite liked the way he leaned toward her, gently and with every thought for her comfort. "My side hurts terribly. Is there something you have that may help?"

Dr. Green nodded at the beautiful young miss before him. She was the loveliest woman he'd ever met, even in her frailty. He watched as her lips moved again, lost in the light blue of her eyes. When she squeezed his hand, he was regretful that he had not been listening. "I am so sorry, Miss, I was not attending. I shall fetch the maid and see that you are given a dose of medicine for your pain."

Anne did not wish for him to leave her side but the pain doubled. Watching his retreating form, she breathed deeply and tried to recall why she was lying in her bed in need of a doctor and feeling so terribly unwell.

In moments, the physician returned with a maid she recognized. She could not sit up but dutifully drank the spoonful's of warm tea that held a slightly bitter taste due to the medicine the doctor had prepared.

He lingered while she drank and Anne allowed herself the liberty of admiring his strong physique when he turned away to place a glass bottle on her bedside table. He was taller than her male cousins but his hair was as fair as her own.

His deep grey eyes were intelligent and kind, full of compassion as he returned his gaze to her face. "I shall go and fetch your mother, Miss de Bourgh."

Anne nodded her head slightly and gave a weak smile to the handsome doctor. "Please, you may call me Anne."

Dr. Green returned her smile. "I shall call you Miss Anne if you insist."

The maid dropped her eyes as Anne finished the

last of her tea and then looked up at the doctor. "Shall I fetch Lady Catherine and Mr. Darcy, sir?"

He seemed to take a moment to register the fact that the maid had addressed him. Anne de Bourgh was a distraction he quite welcomed, but he must take care with appearances where the servants were concerned. "No, you must stay with my patient. I shall send her mother in and then see to Miss Elizabeth."

Anne sat up much too quickly at the mention of her friend. "Is she awake, doctor? When might I see her?"

Before she might swing her feet over the bed, Dr. Green sent the maid from the room and again sat beside his patient. Anne moaned, a hand flying to her side and he helped her to lie back against her pillows. "Oh dear lady, you must not trouble yourself over Miss Elizabeth."

His voice was gentle and so very kind that Anne held onto his hands as he moved to stand. "Do not leave me, doctor, not until the pain has eased. I fear I have never felt such pain."

Lady Catherine's voice carried from the sitting room and the doctor hoped she might lower her tone before entering her daughter's room. Anne de Bourgh closed her eyes and winced as her mother rushed to her side. "Oh my darling! I only went to speak with Darcy in the hallway."

Anne held up a hand to halt her mother's words. "You must not yell, Mother. My hearing was not affected by the accident."

The doctor turned his face away to hide his amusement at Lady Catherine's chastised expression. He stood and waited beside Mr. Darcy as the mistress of Rosings fussed over her daughter.

Anne turned to the gentlemen and sought Darcy's hand. "Fitzwilliam, is Miss Elizabeth well? The doctor mentioned that he would go and sit with her."

Before Mr. Darcy might answer, Lady Catherine stood and glared at Dr. Green. "I cannot think why you mention Elizabeth Bennet to my daughter, sir. As her doctor, you must know we should not overwhelm her with matters that do not pertain to her well-being."

Anne placed a hand to her forehead and Mr. Darcy worried at the expression on her face. She was pale and it was quite obvious she was in pain. "Mother, please, I am not a child. I wish to know how Miss Elizabeth fares. That news would give me much peace."

CHAPTER 12

Dr. Green spoke up, attempting to ease the tension in the room. "Miss Elizabeth has awakened. As far as I can tell, there should be a complete recovery for each of you but we must not force her to recall the accident."

Anne's blue eyes sparkled with unshed tears as she listened to the doctor. "I dreamed of it just now while I slept! Miss Elizabeth and I were together in my gig and I wanted her to come to Rosings. I can't think why now. But it is enough to know she is well. When might I see her?"

Lady Catherine began to argue and Mr. Darcy held up a hand. "Please Aunt Catherine, I am certain the doctor would rather we forego arguments and probing questions for now. In a few days' time, Anne may recall more about all that has happened."

Dr. Green shoved his handkerchief in his breeches pocket and spoke to Anne, ignoring her overbearing mother and thoughtful cousin. "You may see Miss Elizabeth when she is better, my dear. I have instructed one and all that she is to remain at Rosings until she is recovered. Do not worry."

Anne gave a brilliant smile to the man and realized the pain in her side had become bearable. "Thank you, doctor. I appreciate your kindness."

Dr. Green turned reluctantly from the beauty of Anne de Bourgh and nodded to Mr. Darcy and Lady Catherine. "I must go see to Miss Elizabeth and then I shall ride into Hunsford and speak with the apothecary to see if he has any medicine I do not. I'm afraid I left London in such a hurry that I did not think to stop and check my bag thoroughly."

Mr. Darcy bent and placed a light kiss on Anne's forehead. "Rest my dear. I promise I will come sit with you later. Aunt Margaret and Georgie are on their way now to be certain you are well."

Anne's smile gave him much happiness and he turned and gave a look to Lady Catherine. He hoped his eyes conveyed the seriousness of his attitude.

His aunt's expression was one of irritation at having to acquiesce to the doctor's orders. "Go

Fitzwilliam, I promise not to upset my daughter with too many questions."

Mr. Darcy quit Anne's bedchamber and thought of visiting Miss Elizabeth. He did not know whether she would recall his terrible proposal and so he lingered in the hallway instead. He did wish for her to know that her sister Jane would arrive soon as the news was sure to cheer her.

Dr. Green was sitting in a chair beside her bed when Mr. Darcy looked into her room. He was speaking in a low voice. "Miss Elizabeth, how is your pain?"

Mr. Darcy listened intently at the door not wishing to interrupt the interview.

"'Tis better, doctor. I am grateful for your remedy though it was terrible to drink with my tea."

Dr. Green leaned forward and took Elizabeth's hand in his. "I am sorry, my dear. I shall try to make it more palatable after my trip into Hunsford. Perhaps a taste of mint might do the trick?"

Mr. Darcy slowly crossed the space from the door to the bed and stood beside Dr. Green. "I must say it has been a wonderful morning though I would never think a lady injured could ever come to any good. Miss Elizabeth, I wanted to tell you that Miss

Bennet shall arrive soon. Mrs. Collins wrote to her, and to your family, of the accident."

Elizabeth's face was still quite pale but Mr. Darcy's news brought a light to her eyes. "I am quite relieved to know it, Mr. Darcy, thank you. I hate to bother the staff of Rosings."

Dr. Green said his farewells assuring them he would return before dinner.

When he was gone, Mr. Darcy pulled a chair closer to Elizabeth's bedside while the maid remained in the room. The silence between them wore on Mr. Darcy but he would not ask the question he'd longed to ask since she had awakened.

Surely, he thought, *if she remembered my proposal she would send me from this room.*

Eventually Elizabeth bestowed a small smile on the man and sat up slowly as the maid rushed to position her pillows. "Are you sure you ought to sit up, Miss? Dr. Green did say that you were not to tire yourself."

Elizabeth thanked the maid for her kindness. "Please, there is no cause for concern. The pain is not so bad now and I would not go against Dr. Green's wishes."

Mr. Darcy was pleased to see that the lady he knew to be most headstrong and obstinate was behaving with due caution, but he spoke to the maid to reassure her. "I shall sit with her for a while if you must tend Miss Anne. Aunt Catherine mentioned she sent the other maid away."

The young servant curtseyed and gave a start when Lady Catherine's voice boomed in the hallway. "Coming, your ladyship!"

Mr. Darcy stood and followed the servant taking pains to assure that the door of Elizabeth's bedroom remained open. There was little the staff of Rosings might say against him but he wanted Elizabeth to be certain of his intentions.

When he sat again, she looked at him with a bit of curiosity in her gaze. "Mr. Darcy, why do you sit with me if Miss Anne is not well? Both you and the doctor have said there was an accident but I cannot recall it no matter how I try."

Mr. Darcy hoped his expression did not betray his feelings. It seemed Miss Elizabeth did not recall that day and he would not speak on his fears just yet. "My dear cousin is well attended, I assure you. You must know that she was not badly injured so that you do not worry for her."

Elizabeth hugged herself tightly at this news attempting to supply some comfort. "I am relieved to know it. Miss Anne is the last person who ought to have been in an accident. I fear my part in the terrible event," here she paused and gulped hard to steady her voice.

"Mr. Darcy, you may leave me if you wish. You must have business to attend."

Mr. Darcy's heart ached as he watched Miss Elizabeth's attempt at bravery in the face of her confusion. "I would not have you sit here alone until Mrs. Collins or Miss Bennet arrives. It does not seem proper nor kind. As for the accident, I only know that my cousin went out in her gig and did not return. When Richard found her, you were there too. It seems her horse was spooked and you were both thrown from the gig."

Elizabeth's left brow arched at his words. She seemed to contemplate his words for some time before speaking again. "What must Mr. Collins think of my being nursed back to health at Rosings? Surely I must return to the parsonage soon?"

"Dr. Green shall remain at Rosings for a time at my request. With you and Anne in this wing of the house, it makes his job much easier." Mr. Darcy was quite proud of himself for delivering such a logical explanation that the lady could not easily refuse the hospitality of Rosings.

Elizabeth had not thought her injuries to be

serious enough to warrant remaining at Rosings, though her head ached fiercely when she first awoke. The medicine Dr. Green had provided certainly helped but she could not say she felt well. "If you are certain Lady Catherine does not mind, then I shall follow the doctor's orders though I abhor the thought of being a burden to anyone."

Mr. Darcy gazed intently at Elizabeth and fought the urge to take her hand. In spite of her harsh estimation of his character only a few days before, he meant to show her a better side of himself before she might remember all that had passed between them. "Tis not a burden to care for an injured guest for such an estate as Rosings. My aunt is not the most accommodating in her manner, which I am certain you gathered yourself since coming to Kent, but she has been greatly worried for her daughter and so we must forgive her lack of civility."

Smoothing the linen of her borrowed gown, Elizabeth lowered her lashes. "Of course, I imagine she is terribly anxious with Anne in such a state. I must confess that I am most uncomfortable that I cannot recall that day. It leaves me with a terrible feeling I cannot explain but I am most grateful for Dr. Green's presence and the kindness of your family,

Mr. Darcy. I am certain my cousin has made my thanks for me while I was unable."

"Indeed, Mr. Collins is always eager to be certain my aunt knows of his great and lasting appreciation for her benevolence. You must not worry, Miss Elizabeth. In time, your memory may return but until then, you must think only of things that give you peace. Your sister shall make that task easier I hope." Mr. Darcy's eyes were soft with kindness and Elizabeth found relief in his presence. She forced a smile and decided to speak of her silly cousin instead of dwelling on her situation.

"Mr. Collins is a pompous, self-important fellow and as such, a perfect parson for Lady Catherine if you don't mind my saying. Surprisingly, he and Charlotte have made a harmonious marriage that I find gives me much happiness to know after having refused the man," Elizabeth stopped abruptly and covered her mouth, her eyes begging forgiveness.

Mr. Darcy took her hand and gently pulled it from her face. "Do not fear, Miss Elizabeth, you may speak freely with me. I do understand your sentiment for Mr. Collins is not a man one would think of as being a fine husband upon making his acquaintance. But, as they say, reason and love keep little company."

Elizabeth's eyes caught Mr. Darcy's mirth and she squeezed his hand. "Quoting Shakespeare, sir? Are you quite the romantic at heart then? I would hope it to be so for a gentleman must have a bit of poetry in his soul to draw a lady's interest."

Mr. Darcy was surprised by Elizabeth's admission. Only days before she scorned him, but today she seemed to say that she admired him or could admire him. His heart lifted at this notion and he returned the squeeze she had given. "I would count myself most fortunate to have your good opinion Miss Elizabeth. There were moments in the past where I fear I may have drawn your interest for all the wrong reasons."

Elizabeth's brow arched quizzically and she gave a small laugh. "Perhaps the past should stay where it is, Mr. Darcy. People themselves alter so much that there is something new to be observed in them for ever."

Mr. Darcy kept hold of her hand and was delighted by her sentiment. The accident had been a terrible thing but now his true love sat before him smiling and happy to be in his company. It was enough for the day. "And that is a wonderful thought, Miss Elizabeth. One I shall try to recall when I am exasperated with my Aunt Catherine."

Before Elizabeth might make an answer, Charlotte Collins appeared at the door. "Lizzy, the servant sent to the parsonage said you were awake but I feared it might not be true. I have come to sit with you until Jane arrives."

Mr. Darcy stood and pushed the chair away from the bed. "Mrs. Collins, Miss Elizabeth was awakened this morning by Dr. Green and his smelling salts. Better news we could not have!"

Charlotte gave Mr. Darcy a curtsey and stood beside him as they both turned to gaze at Elizabeth. "I am quite thankful to Dr. Green. Is he about? I wish to speak with him."

Mr. Darcy straightened his coat. "He has gone into Hunsford. I am certain you will see him later. He has said we must not expect much from Miss Elizabeth at present as to how the accident occurred. It is best to allow her to recall it naturally to avoid upset and frustration."

Charlotte sat beside Elizabeth and took her hand. "Of course. That is not important at the moment. We must simply provide company and comfort so she may return to good health."

Mr. Darcy was satisfied that Mrs. Collins understood his meaning and turned to quit the room. Elizabeth called to him before he might go. "Mr. Darcy, I am grateful for your company and assurance. You cannot know how you have settled my nerves."

Charlotte turned and looked at Mr. Darcy wondering what had passed between her friend and the proud, handsome man. Before he might go, she stood and walked with him to the door. "Lizzy, I would speak with Mr. Darcy in the hall about Miss Anne for a moment."

Elizabeth nodded and turned to the maid who had come in behind Charlotte and now held a cup of broth for her. The young servant had scurried down to the kitchen after attending Miss Anne and Elizabeth was happy for the comforting aroma of the broth.

Mr. Darcy waited while Charlotte stepped into the hallway before following after her. He glanced to Miss Elizabeth's bed and was pleased to see that she was taking broth. He knew she would be well soon and his joy at that prospect fought with the fear that she would recall her dislike of him before he might have a chance to change her mind.

Charlotte took his arm and walked a few steps down the hallway. "Mr. Darcy, I must tell you now before Lady Catherine appears that Elizabeth told me of her terrible refusal of your proposal. Before Miss Anne arrived at the parsonage that night, Elizabeth knew she had been wrong and was to come to Rosings the next morning to make her apologies. You must not think she was pleased with herself."

Mr. Darcy tried to hide the relief that coursed through his body at these words. "I thank you, Mrs. Collins, for that information. Since it appears Miss Elizabeth does not yet recall much of the accident nor the events of that day, knowing that she does not hate me lifts a burden."

Charlotte meant to say more but Lady Catherine's voice near her daughter's door caused Charlotte to curtsey quickly and hurry back inside Elizabeth's room.

Mr. Darcy moved toward the door to Anne's room in order to keep his aunt from knowing he had just left Miss Elizabeth's room. She met him in a most agitated manner. "Fitzwilliam, my Anne does not seem to understand I must know the reason for her flight from Rosings the other night. Surely you might make her understand that we must know?"

Irritated that his aunt had ignored Dr. Green's directive, Mr. Darcy gave Lady Catherine a stern gaze. "You must not press her, Aunt Catherine. Dr. Green warned you against it did he not?"

The woman gave an exasperated sigh. "I do not care what Dr. Green thinks, Fitzwilliam. I am her mother and as such I know her far better than anyone."

"Be that as it may, she is in pain. You heard her say she dreamed of the accident. I am certain she is only frightened to contemplate that night too deeply at present. Why is it so important that you know all about the accident?" He asked, hoping his aunt would reveal her motive.

"I told you before, Miss Elizabeth Bennet is the cause for my Anne's foolish errand that night. I am certain of it. I will not suffer her presence at Rosings once I have the truth of the matter. Since Miss Elizabeth is awake, she shall tell me what I wish to know!" Lady Catherine turned toward Elizabeth's door and Mr. Darcy grabbed her shoulder before he might stop himself.

"There is no need for such theatrics! Miss Elizabeth cannot recall a thing from that night and I won't have you interrogating her as though she is some criminal!"

Lady Catherine pulled free of her nephew's grasp and drew up to her full height. Her expression was one of disdain but there was a hint of curiosity in her tone. "How would you know what she might recall? Surely you have not been sitting by her side all this time?"

Mr. Darcy would not deny his visit. "I sat with her until Mrs. Collins came. 'Tis cruel to leave her all alone in her condition."

Lady Catherine was not appeased. "Mark my words, I will not tolerate such a horrible young woman in my house a moment longer than necessary. Your concern for her is appalling seeing you are promised to my Anne."

Moving to stand between his aunt and Elizabeth's door, Mr. Darcy spoke his mind without attempt to temper his words. "My kindness to a lady of my acquaintance is all that is proper. My only concern is that she is restored to good health."

Lying so to his aunt gave a sting to his conscious, for his concern was that he might start anew with Miss Elizabeth and gain her approval especially after the news Charlotte Collins had shared with him. But his meddlesome aunt would not be so easily deterred.

"I meant what I said. Once the young lady is recovered, she will leave Rosings. In the meantime, you must give your attention to Anne for she is to be your wife one day. The staff will gossip if you are often in the room of our guest."

With that, Lady Catherine led him inside Anne's suite of rooms to be certain he did her bidding.

CHAPTER 13

THE NEXT DAY, Lady Catherine sat in the parlor with Mr. Darcy and Colonel Fitzwilliam while Anne de Bourgh was occupied with Dr. Green and Elizabeth Bennet in her own sitting room upstairs. The ladies were playing a game with cards the doctor had developed to test memory in a passive manner.

Colonel Fitzwilliam stood and paced for the second time in less than half an hour when the noise of an arrival drifted from the entryway through the open parlor door. "It must be Mother and James at last. I shall go to meet them," he said as he hastened from the room.

The entryway was much preferred to the parlor as his Aunt Catherine had spent the better part of an hour enumerating the failings of Miss Elizabeth Bennet. How Darcy could stand it he did not know, but his own patience was worn so thin as to be nearly gone.

As Lady Matlock stepped through the door behind his brother, Colonel Fitzwilliam went to her without having to pretend at happiness. Her presence would be a welcome distraction and perhaps ease his Aunt Catherine's anger.

Georgiana Darcy entered behind his mother. The young mistress of Pemberley relied upon himself and Darcy as her guardians though it had been many months since he'd shared the burden equally with his cousin.

When she saw Richard, she gave a squeal and hurried into his arms. He was her favorite gentleman in all the world besides her brother. "Oh, Richard, you are as handsome as ever though I'd nearly forgotten your face after all this time."

Sweeping his charge into his arms, Richard twirled her in an impromptu dance about the entryway as Mr. Darcy emerged from the parlor at the noise his sister and cousin made.

As he brought Georgiana back to stand beside his mother, Richard's breath was taken by the fair haired beauty who entered last of all. Miss Jane Bennet's cheeks held the slightest tinge of pink as the skirt of her dress was ruffled by a gust of spring air that swirled into the entryway.

Richard Fitzwilliam stood speechless as the woman moved closer to his mother, her eyes glancing to his face before finding the floor.

"Miss Bennet," his mother said as Mr. Darcy engaged in conversation with his sister and cousin James, "this is my youngest son, Colonel Richard Fitzwilliam."

Jane lifted her gaze and gave a beautiful smile to the tall, handsome man she had come to know through Miss Darcy's tales throughout their trip from London.

She held out a gloved hand and made a small curtsey before speaking, "I am pleased to make your acquaintance at last, sir. I am told you were the one who found my sister and Miss de Bourgh after their accident. I am quite thankful for your kindness and diligence in seeing my sister safely to Rosings."

Richard cleared his throat and pushed away thoughts of tracing the perfect bow of her bottom lip with his thumb. It required a great deal of his composure but he took her hand and gave a slight bow over it. "It is I who am pleased to make your acquaintance, Miss Bennet. I ought to have known you were related to Miss Elizabeth the moment you entered

Rosings for you do favor her in looks though fairer, I must say."

Jane's blush deepened as Lady Matlock took her youngest son's arm and steered him toward the parlor instructing James to escort their traveling companion while Mr. Darcy waited with Georgiana to be the last to enter the parlor.

James Fitzwilliam smiled at Jane and offered his arm. He was on friendly terms with the eldest Bennet daughter after their travels from London but could see that his younger brother seemed taken with the woman. "Do be careful of my brother, Miss Bennet, he is a notorious lady's man. A breaker of hearts, if you will."

Jane laughed with James and shook her head. "I am here to return my sister to good health, sir, and nothing more I assure you."

Mr. Darcy spoke as James approached with Jane. "Miss Bennet, I am pleased you have come. Miss Elizabeth is sitting with Cousin Anne in her parlor upstairs. Would you care to join them?"

Knowing she must first see Lady Catherine, though she dreaded the very idea, Jane thanked Mr. Darcy again for his kindness. "I would love nothing more than to fly to my sister's side but it would be rude not to make the acquaintance of Lady Catherine de Bourgh first."

Mr. Darcy nodded and James led Jane into the parlor for the meeting with the mistress of Rosings. As they gained the parlor door, he whispered in confidence to his nervous partner. "Do not fret, Miss Bennet. Aunt Catherine is a fearsome lady, but with all of us present to distract her you may slip away as soon as she begins to berate Mother for only paying a visit when tragedy strikes."

Jane breathed a deep sigh of relief at James's words and walked forward with her escort to give her thanks to the woman who had provided aid and comfort to her sister.

When the introduction was made, Lady Catherine eyed her with a cold disdain that made Jane tremble. The chill breeze that had swept in with her when she entered the home was warm in comparison to the woman's gaze.

Hoping to soon hurry upstairs to her sister, Jane smiled at the formidable mistress of Rosings. "I've told Mr. Darcy of my family's great debt to you for your kindness, your ladyship, but I would be remiss if I did not give my thanks, and that of my parents, to you now. We are most humbled by your generosity and kindness in my sister's time of need."

Lady Catherine gave a dismissive wave of her hand. "What else would you expect from a peer with proper breeding and common sense, Miss Bennet? Surely in your own county the gentlefolk can be relied upon to shelter those less fortunate even if their connections are lacking?"

Jane bit her tongue to keep the impertinent words that leapt to mind locked in her throat. Elizabeth's letters describing the haughty and overly confident woman had done little to prepare her for the stinging reality of standing in her presence.

Mr. Darcy drew his aunt's attention by stunning the entire party. "Aunt Catherine! Please attempt to show humility and courtesy to our guest. She has been nothing but kind to stop and speak with you when her greatest desire is to dash upstairs and see her sister."

Lady Catherine turned her fury upon her nephew and James winked at Jane. He moved to stand in front of her and Jane did not tarry as she moved to the door of the parlor.

As soon as she gained the entryway, Jane stopped and leaned against the dark wood paneling that gleamed richly from having been polished day after day, year after year, by servants who likely received the same bitterness Jane had been subjected to in the parlor. As her father said many times, the world was often blind to the offenses of those with rank and money.

Jane pushed away from the paneled wall and gained the first step of the grand stairway thinking if she were ever to marry into a wealthy family she would always consider her words and their weight on the hearts of those who might serve her.

Forgetting Lady Catherine's prickly demeanor, she hurried up the stairs not caring that she did not know which rooms Miss de Bourgh and Elizabeth occupied. Surely a maid would come along and send her on her way sooner or later.

In any event, it was delightful to wander the halls of Rosings with their royal blue carpeting and exquisite paintings that glimmered in the flickering candlelight.

Returning to the top of the staircase after having walked the length of one hallway and hearing not a sound that might be attributed to her sister, Jane peered to her right and decided to stretch her legs in that direction when a maid appeared from a doorway halfway down that same hallway.

Upon seeing Jane, the maid quickened her pace and soon stood before Jane and made her inquiry. "Excuse me, miss, are you lost?"

Jane smiled at the fresh face of the young servant happy to see that at least she had not yet been cowed by her employer. "I am. My name is Jane Bennet and I have come with the Matlocks to see my sister, Elizabeth Bennet. She was injured a few days ago."

The maid nodded her head and stepped aside. "Oh yes, Miss Bennet, your sister is with Miss Anne in her rooms. Dr. Green is with them now but I can take you there if you like."

Quite liking the young woman's friendly demeanor, Jane nodded and followed her down the hallway. "Who is Dr. Green?"

The young maid smiled. "He is the physician come from London at Mr. Darcy's request. He was able to awaken Miss Elizabeth, oh and he is the most handsome fellow. But please, do not let on that I said so for I am certain her ladyship would have me returned to the kitchens did she know it."

Jane placed a hand on the maid's slender arm. "You must not worry on my account. I would never wish to see anyone stand before Lady Catherine to be found wanting as I did a few moments ago."

The maid giggled as Jane's description of her arrival. "Oh, Miss Bennet, do not worry over her greeting. Mr. Darcy will not allow her to do more than hurl words your way. He stood up to her and demanded Miss Elizabeth be given the room next to Miss Anne. You ought to have seen it! I think he might be in love with your sister for he never leaves her side for long and will not allow his aunt to bedevil her in the least."

Jane gasped at the maid's knowledge of the intimate workings above stairs and the feelings Mr. Darcy held for her sister. Elizabeth had not mentioned any great fondness for him in her letters. She wondered what had happened while her sister had been a guest at the parsonage.

The maid pushed open the door to Miss Anne's sitting room and Jane rushed inside when she heard Elizabeth's laughter. Surely she must be well to laugh so with her usual mirth.

When Elizabeth saw Jane, she jumped up much too quickly and lost her balance for a moment. Dr. Green nearly vaulted over the table between the sofa and the chair where he had been seated.

Steadying Elizabeth and turning to Jane, he gave a tight smile before settling Elizabeth back on the sofa beside Miss Anne. "Young lady, you must not cause such excitement for our patient."

Jane rushed to Elizabeth's side mumbling her apologies to the doctor. "I am sorry, sir, but I heard her laughter and it was as I remembered before the accident. I thought she must be well."

Elizabeth swiped at the tears that came unbidden and reached out for her sister. "Oh, Jane, I am not well. Not at all. Dr. Green is right, I must not leave just yet. Have you come to stay with me?"

"Yes, my dear, indeed I have. You must not worry for our lodgings at present. Mr. Darcy has assured me you shall remain here until you are recovered. There is no rush. I shall not return to London without you."

Elizabeth's eyes glistened with unshed tears as Jane pulled her close. They had always been one another's favorite and now that Jane had finally arrived at Rosings, she would see to it that her dearest sister was happy and whole again.

CHAPTER 14

Mr. Darcy was eager to quit the parlor and leave the vicious complaints of his Aunt Catherine behind. But Georgiana was seated happily beside him and he could not countenance separating himself from her so soon after her arrival.

James and Richard stood by the fireplace and held their own conversation as Lady Matlock attempted time and again to distract the mistress of Rosings. "Catherine, surely they are not so bad as all that. Miss Jane Bennet was quite a lovely traveling companion and Georgie has made a friendship with the woman."

Lady Catherine cast a severe eye to her spoiled niece at this admission from Lady Matlock. "Because your brother and Richard are unable to provide the proper companions and direction, I shall

138

have to see to it myself while you are here young lady."

Georgiana's cheeks flamed a bright red and she turned to Mr. Darcy with tears glistening in her eyes. Rising swiftly to his feet and offering his arm to his sister, Mr. Darcy fixed his aunt with a withering gaze. "Aunt Catherine, you are being most unkind to not only my dear sister but to the young ladies above stairs who have done nothing to gain such censure."

Lady Catherine rapped her cane upon the floor as Mr. Darcy turned to quit the parlor with Georgiana. "See here, nephew! It is by your tender mercies Miss Elizabeth remains in my home. I am beginning to wonder why you hold such interest in her recovery."

The air in the room grew heavy as Mr. Darcy turned to face the hateful woman he could in no way connect with his own dear departed mother. How they came from the same family he could not fathom.

"Aunt Catherine, the depths to which you continually sink ought to have prepared me for such vulgar behavior today but I would remind you that my personal business is not up for discussion. I've half a mind to remove the Bennet sisters and my own family from Rosings today and return to Pemberley. As it stands, Miss Elizabeth is not well enough to travel. From this moment forth, you will not address me on the matter."

Turning and escorting his sister from the room, Mr. Darcy ignored the high pitched voice of his aunt as she heaped condemnation upon him. His heart was stricken by the disparaging remarks of his aunt toward his beloved. In Miss Elizabeth's estimation, he had behaved in much the same manner towards her family and herself when he gave what he had thought to be a most heartfelt proposal.

What a fool he had been! Never would he think himself equal to his Aunt Catherine and her terrible disdain and less than charitable prejudices, but it seemed he had taken more of her personality than that of his own mother.

Georgiana spoke and startled him from his bleak reverie. "Brother, I cannot understand why Aunt Catherine is so unkind. If you care so for Miss Elizabeth, she cannot be such a terrible lady. Why her sister was most kind and truly a friend to me as we traveled from London."

Mr. Darcy smiled and led his sister up the stairs. "She is a lovely lady, Georgie. It is only that her connections are not the kind those of our circle would approve. Just as you have rightly judged Miss

Bennet, you will soon see that her sister possesses a gracious manner and a sparkling wit."

Georgiana was pleased by her brother's words. "Miss Bennet is a lovely young lady and so Miss Elizabeth must be as well. I trust your judgment far more than Aunt Catherine's and so I shall believe Miss Elizabeth innocent of all charges against her."

Mr. Darcy's eyes shone with the pride he always felt for his younger sister. She was still quite young and had not always been a great judge of character, though the incident with Wickham at Ramsgate was hardly her fault.

He would see to it that she became better acquainted with the woman he hoped would soon join their family. "Come along, I am certain Anne will be pleased to see you at last. We shall have tea in her sitting room and hopefully Aunt Catherine shall remain downstairs with Aunt Margaret."

Upon entering Anne's suite of rooms, Georgiana grew happy once more and hurried to her cousin's side. "Oh, Anne, I have been so worried but you seem to be well!"

Anne de Bourgh patted the seat beside her. "Come sit, Georgie, there is much to tell. I am better than yesterday though I try not to think of the accident so much."

Mr. Darcy took a seat in the chair next to Dr. Green and thanked the man for his care of the young ladies. "I say, Green, my cousin and Miss Elizabeth do appear well. Had we not received your guidance I would think them recovered."

Dr. Green looked to his patients with a keen eye. "Yes, they are both in much better spirits gathered together in this room. I think the company and light conversation is a good tonic."

Mr. Darcy gazed at Miss Elizabeth without attempting to hide his feelings. Seeing her seated before him with the bloom in her cheeks and the smile her sister Jane had brought was surely the happiest moment of his life. "I thank you, Green. Your excellent care has been duly noted and I wish for you to send notice to my townhouse on Grosvenor when you have returned to London. I shall cover the cost for the care of both young ladies as my Aunt Catherine should not be bothered."

The doctor did not like to speak of payment in the company of his patients but Mr. Darcy had kept his voice low enough that the ladies had not heard. "Tis my pleasure to serve the Darcy family, sir. I only wish I might stay longer to see that both young ladies are well, but I fear I must return to Town at the end of my fortnight."

Mr. Darcy waved to his cousin's maid as the servant entered the sitting room. "Please see that tea is brought to us here."

Turning to Dr. Green, he settled himself in the comfort of the silk upholstered chair and assured the man that he would write to him of his patients. "You may write to me here, Green. I plan to stay until I am certain they are recovered and see the Bennet sisters back to London. Perhaps you might visit with Miss Elizabeth there?"

Dr. Green gave a satisfied smile. "That would ease my conscience Mr. Darcy. If only it would be so easy to see Miss Anne again."

Mr. Darcy wondered at the tone that crept into the man's voice as he spoke of Anne. Had the physician grown fond of his cousin so soon? Or was it merely concern for her health?

Instead of questioning the doctor on the matter, Mr. Darcy listened as Green spoke of cases where memory had returned to his patients gradually over many months while others seemed to be coaxed forth by a sound, an odor, or a familiar setting or conversation. "The mind is a powerful thing, Mr. Darcy. Far more than we realize at times. Still, I think it best for patients to recover in their own time without prompting. In this particular case, I believe Miss Elizabeth shall benefit from keeping company with Miss Anne as she did before the accident."

Elizabeth, hearing the physician's words, turned her gaze from Jane and the other two ladies when tea arrived and seemed to be daydreaming as she stared at Mr. Darcy.

The gentleman openly returned her gaze, the beginnings of a smile playing on his lips. Before she might turn away, Mr. Darcy spoke as the maid poured tea for the party. "Miss Elizabeth, did you wish to speak with me?"

Elizabeth's brow arched and she smiled at Mr. Darcy. "I only wanted to thank you for having Jane brought swiftly from London. You cannot know what a comfort it is to have her by my side."

Mr. Darcy took his teacup and allowed the smile that teased the corner of his mouth to blossom fully as he looked upon his beloved. "'Tis my pleasure, Miss Elizabeth. Having Georgie by my side is always a great comfort to me and so I do understand the sentiment."

As the hour passed, Elizabeth glanced several times more in Mr. Darcy's direction and the man thought he detected a hint of curiosity in her gaze. He wondered what she thought of him now. He'd give anything to be privy to the thoughts that lurked behind her fine eyes.

Anne de Bourgh's eyes flitted from her handsome cousin to Miss Elizabeth as Georgiana spoke with Dr. Green. In a moment, before she could guard her thoughts, Anne recalled standing before the library door and overhearing Darcy as he told Richard of his proposal to Miss Elizabeth and her refusal.

She bit her bottom lip to keep from gasping aloud and drawing attention to herself. Her mad dash from Rosings to the parsonage had been for her cousin, to fix his proposal and bring Miss Elizabeth to him so that they might be married! Turning back to Georgiana, Miss Anne began to think of how she might push Miss Elizabeth toward her cousin.

Across from the ladies on the sofa, Mr. Darcy watched the Bennet sisters and felt pricked in his heart by guilt and regret. He had never intended offense when he proposed to the impertinent lass of Longbourn but intentions were a small comfort when faced with the truth of the matter. He was as proud and carried as much prejudice as his aunt. What would his mother think of him were she alive today?

He looked to Georgie, admiring her fair head

bent close to Anne's with giggles passing between them. They both favored his mother and he knew he must behave in a more gentlemanlike manner in the future, for them as well as for Miss Elizabeth.

If happiness were to be within his grasp again, Mr. Darcy knew he must humble himself.

CHAPTER 15

Lady Catherine remained in the parlor with Lady Matlock and her Fitzwilliam nephews after Darcy had taken Georgiana upstairs to see Anne. "He is making a grave mistake, Margaret, and I am disappointed Richard has not steered him away from the Bennet family."

Richard Fitzwilliam stared at his Aunt Catherine in a state of mild concern. Surely she had not learned of Darcy's failed proposal? He knew Miss Elizabeth had not recalled anything of the accident and to his knowledge, he was the only other person to know of Darcy's secret.

He stood and walked to the fireplace to stand beside his brother. James shook his head as their mother tried to reason with their aunt. "What is she on about now, Richard? Why would you need to warn Darcy away from the Bennets?"

Richard shrugged his shoulders and tried to swallow the guilt at lying to his brother. "You know Aunt Catherine as well as I. She has it in her mind that Darcy, in his kindness for an acquaintance, holds some hidden motive in regard to Miss Elizabeth. She cannot accept that her daughter has a mind of her own and will not tell her why she left Rosings that night, either."

James drank deeply from his glass of port before placing it upon the mantel. "I do hope that Mother is able to distract her. Darcy will not hesitate to remove to Pemberley and then poor Anne would be left all alone in her recovery."

Richard knew Darcy might do just as his brother feared. If so, he must take what opportunity presented itself to deepen his acquaintance with the lovely Jane Bennet before she was whisked out of his life.

Taking his brother's glass, he nodded toward the door of the parlor. "Let us retire to the library and allow Mother to settle Aunt Catherine's nerves. I would like to know how things are coming along with Miss Cort. Have you proposed yet?"

James smirked at his brother. "Let us speak of it in the library, Richard."

The brothers went to their mother and Aunt Catherine and made their apologies. Richard kissed his mother's forehead and squeezed the hand she offered. "We must visit later for James and I have much to discuss since last we met. Perhaps a wedding shall soon be held at our estate in Derbyshire?"

Lady Matlock glanced at her eldest son. "I expect as soon as we return to London there shall be an engagement ball. Now, off with the both of you."

When her nephews had quit the parlor, Lady Catherine continued her tirade. "Mark my words, Margaret, I will see that Darcy makes his intentions clear toward my Anne before this visit has come to an end. She has waited far too long as it stands."

Lady Matlock attempted to address the truth of the matter though she knew it would anger Lady Catherine. "I cannot imagine that you still believe Fitzwilliam and Anne shall be wed. You know well that she cannot bear him an heir. How might the master of Pemberley agree to such a thing while he is yet a young and virile man?"

Lady Catherine's anger increased tenfold at the words she knew very well to be true. "It matters little to me whether Anne is able to provide an heir. Georgiana shall certainly marry well and provide several children to carry on at Pemberley and his other estates."

Margaret Fitzwilliam did not hide her shock for a moment though she knew there was no reasoning with the haughty woman before her. "How terrible to wish for Darcy to live such an existence! Neither he nor Anne hold any desire for one another and you must let the matter drop before you drive him away for good."

"I will not! I'm telling you, there is something about Miss Elizabeth Bennet and that is why he has turned his attention from my Anne. The woman has wormed her way into this house by drawing my own daughter out into the cold of the evening and now has got what she wanted. Well, I will not abide it I tell you!"

Lady Matlock stood and shook her head at the senseless woman who was her sister by marriage. "Catherine, as ever, you waste precious little time in reminding me of the reasons we rarely make the trip to Kent. I would retire before dinner and offer you my best piece of advice. Do not push Darcy on this matter, for he will leave and Anne will be the one to suffer alone in her recovery."

Lady Catherine carried on with her strident complaints as Lady Matlock quit the parlor. As the mother of Richard and James Fitzwilliam gained the stairs, she thought of returning to sit with the bitter old woman she avoided whenever possible as it was likely that Anne's injury had simply pushed her past all common sense and restraint.

Instead, she thought of whether Catherine might be onto something where Miss Bennet's sister and her nephew were concerned. Turning to make her way to the library, Margaret Fitzwilliam resolved to find whether Richard held any knowledge of an attraction between the pair.

James and Richard raised their heads as one and glanced toward the door as their mother tapped upon the heavy polished wood. "Come in," James called as Richard gave a heavy sigh.

When his mother entered, he and his brother stood but Richard's spirits did not lift for he knew she must have been influenced by his Aunt Catherine's tirade. "Mother, she must be in rare form indeed if you have left the comfort of the parlor to seek shelter amongst your sons in the smoke of the library."

He lowered his cigar and glanced to James. Both knew their mother despised the smell but would never chastise their father in his own library. Here at Rosings, however, she was likely to fuss at her sons over the indulgence.

Instead, she made herself comfortable on the sofa across the way and looked from one son to the other. "How I wish our dear Anne had not been injured. I would not come to Kent again if we might avoid it."

James sat and placed his cigar on the edge of the table beside him out of respect for his mother's abhorrence of the habit. "Mother, surely we might return to Town since we have delivered Miss Bennet and Georgie? Stay a day or so and pamper Anne until you are satisfied she is well and then we may all leave for Town."

Colonel Fitzwilliam spoke in favor of staying at Rosings for a time as he would like to become better acquainted with Miss Bennet. "Surely we might suffer Aunt Catherine's company in order to lift poor Anne's spirits? James, you might be so kind as to go out on the morrow and see to the spring planting. You shall be in charge of the estate in Derbyshire someday and now's a good a time as any to practice the management of lands."

James gave his brother a sour look that turned into a sincere expression of alarm as his mother agreed. "It would be nice for your Aunt Catherine to feel as though there was some other use for her time than cutting down the Bennet sisters, James. I shall tell her over dinner of your plans."

Turning to her youngest son, Lady Matlock pinned him with her gaze. Richard puffed his cigar contentedly as he did not share his brother's worry over their mother's dislike of the thing. "I believe you might have some knowledge of why Catherine believes there is some connection between Darcy and Miss Elizabeth."

Richard was not easily cowed by his mother. He was a military man after all and not given to revealing all that he knew unless there was ample reason to divulge the secrets entrusted to him. "Mother, Darcy is a gentleman above all else. He first made Miss Elizabeth's acquaintance in Hertford-shire while helping Bingley with some estate in the countryside. Of course he felt a responsibility for Miss Elizabeth when she was brought home with Anne in a wagon the other night."

Hoping his omission of the truth would not count as a lie, Richard simply watched his mother's eyes to see whether she believed his dismissal of Lady Catherine's suspicions.

Relieved when at last she came to bid him and James a good night, Richard stood and received her embrace. "I am so happy to see you again that this time I shall choose to accept your explanation instead of chasing after Catherine's outlandish suspicions. Though I do wonder how the two young ladies came to be together upon the road."

Lady Matlock moved away and hugged his brother and Richard held the relief that flooded his body in check until she'd quit the library. His brother, however, had not bought the story and when they sat again with cigars in hand, James questioned him.

"I know when you are scheming Richard and I suspect it has much more to do with Miss Bennet than Darcy and her sister, but let me advise you where the beautiful lady is concerned. Mother and Father have not pressed you as to your marital plans because of my coming engagement to Miss Cort, but know that you must marry a young lady of means as well. As lovely as Miss Bennet is, and I would heartily approve of her as a sister, she has not the dowry to satisfy our parents."

Richard nodded as his brother finished his speech but kept his counsel. He would never have believed in love at first sight before meeting the lovely sister of Miss Elizabeth this very day but Miss

Bennet was a lady he could spend his life with, of that he was certain.

The Bennet sisters might not be considered as suitable matches by Aunt Catherine and his parents, but he knew Darcy cared as little for their opinion as he found himself caring at the moment.

Stretching to enjoy the luxurious depth of his chair, Richard smirked at his brother and lifted his glass in a toast. "Love sought is good, but given unsought is better."

James lifted his glass and laughed at Richard. "Take care, brother, or I might assume that the lady has already claimed your heart."

CHAPTER 16

ELIZABETH BENNET SAT on the bed in her room at Rosings with Jane by her side. The home had become full with guests and she was pleased her sister was among them. "Oh, Jane, I could not wish for a better nurse than you. The maids and Charlotte have been most attentive and while I am grateful for their care, there is none like you."

Jane scooted closer to Elizabeth and hugged her for the tenth time since she had found her dearest sister upstairs at Rosings. "I left London as soon as I was able, the very afternoon the express arrived from Rosings. Aunt Madeline and Uncle Edward send their love and would make the trip if I write and tell them they must come."

Elizabeth knew her relations in Cheapside

would have brought Jane to Kent had the Matlocks not extended their invitation. "You must write them on the morrow and say I am well. I am, Jane, except that I cannot recall why I was in that gig with Miss Anne. I suppose there is a very good reason but no one seems to know."

"I would not worry, Lizzy, for it could not be so important if neither of you recall it now. At some time in the future it may become clear but your recovery is more important, I think." Jane smoothed her skirts and smiled encouragingly at Elizabeth.

"You are ever the practical one Jane. I do remember your letters and after speaking with Colonel Fitzwilliam, I found quite by accident that Mr. Darcy was the one to warn Mr. Bingley away in Hertfordshire. Can you imagine?"

Jane frowned and took Elizabeth's hand. "Let me put this to rest once and for all, Lizzy. Mr. Bingley is not the man I once thought him to be. I have left the notion of becoming Mrs. Bingley behind and I wish you would do so as well. Let us speak of Colonel Fitzwilliam instead."

Elizabeth laughed and watched her sister's cheeks as a lovely pink blush stole across them. "Do you mean to say you would like for me to tell you all about the man, to satisfy your interest in him? You can't have spent more than a few minutes in his presence earlier."

Jane stood and crossed the room to stand before the dressing table. "Come sit before the mirror and let me fix your hair. I can see it's been some time since it was given a proper brushing."

Laughing again, Elizabeth touched her hair before standing slowly to follow her sister to the ornate dressing table by one of the large windows that looked out over the rose garden. Even now she longed to walk its paths and escape the four walls of her room. Sitting so that Jane might attend her, Elizabeth determined she would seek Dr. Green's permission for a short walk on the morrow.

As Jane hummed a happy tune, Elizabeth took up their conversation once more. "Colonel Fitzwilliam is a kind man with a wonderful sense of humor. Where Mr. Darcy is taciturn, the Colonel has an easy manner in conversation. I often find myself wishing Mr. Darcy shared his friendly nature but he does possess his own charm of a kind, I suppose."

Jane was astonished by Elizabeth's words regarding Mr. Darcy. "Lizzy, I am surprised to hear you speak well of Mr. Darcy. The air in Kent must have softened your attitude where he is concerned. The maid that brought me to you when I first arrived did speculate that Mr. Darcy may have feelings for you. Love, I think it was she said when telling me how he defends you against his Aunt Catherine's anger."

Elizabeth's mouth dropped open at this news. "I cannot think why the maid would be so impertinent! Mr. Darcy has been nothing but a proper gentleman all this time. Do you think the maid would say such to anyone else at Rosings?"

Jane continued to brush her sister's hair while considering Elizabeth's reply. "I doubt she would with Lady Catherine so set against us. She was horrible in the parlor when first we met, Lizzy. I could not have known she was as terrible as you said in your letters without having met her myself. Mr. Darcy did defend us before I left the parlor. Perhaps the maid is correct after all?"

Elizabeth would not admit that her heart leapt at the idea of Mr. Darcy being in love with her. It was simply foolish to think of it. "Perhaps it is only the gossip of a romantic, Jane. In any case, we were discussing Colonel Fitzwilliam and he is a handsome man who might sweep you off your feet before we return to London. I would not be sad to see you become better acquainted."

Knowing her sister was turning the conversation back to the Colonel to avoid further discussion of Mr. Darcy, Jane indulged the talk of Richard Fitzwilliam. "There is something about him and in the entryway earlier, I felt as though we were meant to meet."

"How terribly romantic Jane! Perhaps circumstances have transpired to bring the two of you together. I can say this without a doubt, he is a much better man than Charles Bingley."

Jane stopped her brushing and gave her sister such a look at this proclamation that Elizabeth was immediately sorry for having brought up the man's name. "Do not stop brushing just yet, sister. I promise never to speak of that man again if you will only forgive me."

Resuming the gentle strokes of the brush, Jane gave Elizabeth a small smile and spoke again of Colonel Fitzwilliam. "I will not fall so easily this time, Lizzy. Though the butterflies in my stomach earlier when we met were such a surprise, I will not pin my hopes on the smiles and compliments of a man I do not know well."

Elizabeth listened carefully to her sister's words

and realized that Jane had developed a picture of the man in her mind while traveling to Kent with his family that was likely influenced by their feelings for the man.

If Jane found happiness with Richard Fitzwilliam, Elizabeth would think her accident worth the pain but certainly there were easier ways to introduce a sister to the handsome second son of an Earl.

Finally leaving Elizabeth to dress for dinner, Jane slipped away to her own room across the hall. Miss Darcy insisted they have rooms next to one another as she had grown quite fond of Jane.

The young mistress of Pemberley was a lonely girl though she was not secluded at her family's estate in the same way as Miss de Bourgh was at Rosings. Jane thought it terribly sad that the two young ladies did not reside nearer to one other. There was little doubt in her mind they would both benefit from such an arrangement.

When she thought of living a life all alone on a large estate without a sibling, her heart ached. Again, Jane thought when she married she would never have only one child or children so far apart in age they would never know one another well.

Laughing at herself as she stood outside the door

to her room as Elizabeth's maid brought her trunk behind her, Jane was startled to see Colonel Fitzwilliam approaching from the other end of the hallway. He must be coming to visit Miss de Bourgh.

When he saw Jane, he smiled and called out to her. Not knowing what to do other than acknowledge the man's presence, Jane schooled her face and waited for him.

Her heart dipped and the butterflies returned as the man stopped before her. Jane bit her bottom lip and clasped her hands behind her. An overwhelming urge to disappear into her room struck and Jane stammered helplessly. "I...I am sorry, Colonel, I...I must dress for dinner."

She turned away and entered the room before he might speak. Richard was baffled by her actions and moved to stand in the doorway. "Miss Bennet, please forgive me. I did not mean to cause you alarm."

Jane was mortified by her actions and grasped the door knob tightly before she might throw herself into his arms not caring whether the maid saw. Breathing deeply to calm herself, she managed to smooth away his fears. "Do not mind me, I fear I am quite tired after our trip and seeing my sister. Please forgive me."

Richard nodded and stepped away from the

door. "I understand. I look forward to seeing you at dinner if you are able to come down."

Jane watched as he turned and continued further down the hallway. She wanted to run after him and explain that she was not tired, that the problem was only that he took her breath away. Instead, she slowly closed the door and turned to the waiting maid.

"Shall I unpack your trunk, Miss Bennet, and then help you dress for dinner?"

Smiling at the young servant, Jane moved to the bed and ran a hand along the exquisite quilt that lay across the bottom. "No thank you, I would lie down for I am truly tired."

The maid curtseyed and quit the room and Jane pushed a breath of relief from her lungs. Instead of lying down, she moved to her trunk and began to unpack her things as she thought of dining with the handsome cousin of Mr. Darcy.

It was foolish to allow herself to become so enamored with a man she barely knew. Hadn't she done the same with Charles Bingley? She had made Elizabeth promise not to speak of the man and here she was thinking of him. But Richard Fitzwilliam was not Mr. Bingley and she was not foolish to be attracted to a handsome man who might return her feelings. Still, caution was due where her heart was concerned.

Finishing her unpacking and making her way to the bed, Jane allowed herself to daydream about a life with Richard Fitzwilliam despite her resolve to go slow.

CHAPTER 17

THE NEXT DAY, Dr. Green approved of Elizabeth's plan to have the young people of Rosings take a turn about the gardens as the sun was shining brightly and the chill of winter had finally given way to spring.

As Miss Darcy took James Fitzwilliam's arm, Dr. Green moved to stand beside Miss de Bourgh. Elizabeth noticed the young woman's eyes and the way they rested on the doctor's face. Something was stirring between the pair and Elizabeth hoped Lady Catherine would not see it for herself.

Mr. Darcy offered his arm and Elizabeth glanced at him for a moment too long. She watched as his Adam's apple bobbed in this throat before placing her hand on his arm. She thought he looked at her the same way Miss Anne had looked at Dr. Green. Could Mr. Darcy be in love with her?

The very idea startled her and she looked quickly away in time to see Colonel Fitzwilliam approach Jane. At dinner the evening before, the two had been seated with Miss Anne between them and Elizabeth had not missed the stolen glances back and forth.

She had been seated between James Fitzwilliam and his mother while Mr. Darcy sat near the mistress of Rosings. It had been a lovely dinner and her conversation with Mr. Darcy's Fitzwilliam relations had been much more solicitous than any conversation she'd had with Lady Catherine. In them, she could see that Mr. Darcy's entire family was not of the same temperament as the grand lady of Rosings.

Now as the party of four couples entered the gardens, Elizabeth breathed deeply of the fresh air and allowed her eyes to roam freely about the grounds taking in every sight and sound as though she might never see them again. She had been trapped inside for so many days!

Her head ached only slightly but she would not have missed the opportunity to wander the grounds. While her room was splendidly decorated and most comfortable, the richly papered walls seemed a prison to one who was accustomed to walking each day.

To think of Miss de Bourgh spending her life cloistered inside those same walls sent a tremble through Elizabeth's body. Being the daughter of a gentleman on a lovely yet humble estate was not such a terrible thing when one considered how lonely a young woman could be with all the wealth of the world at her disposal.

As she watched her sister with Colonel Fitzwilliam, Mr. Darcy spoke and Elizabeth found herself eager to hear what he had to say. "'Tis a lovely day for a walk about the grounds. Have you been to Kent before Miss Elizabeth? They say there are no better gardens in all of England."

Elizabeth remembered her arrival in Kent with the Lucases and a thoughtful expression appeared on her face. "I don't believe I have ever been to Kent before, Mr. Darcy. I only came this one time to visit Charlotte and my cousin. I must agree that the gardens here are the loveliest in memory."

Mr. Darcy's expression was pained and he stopped their progress. Turning to her, his eyes soft with concern, he placed his warm hand on top of hers. "I must apologize, Miss Elizabeth. I did not mean to bring up the past. It can't be right to ask you to recall where you have been."

Elizabeth smiled brightly, hoping to ease his fears. "I am no frail young lady you must fear upsetting. While I may not recall much of the accident, I do know who I am and where I have been in my lifetime. Please do not take care with your words. Treat me as you always have before."

She was surprised when the man began their walk again without speaking further. He seemed to ponder all that she'd said and Elizabeth hoped she had not offended him.

After several steps, he turned to her with a regretful grin. "Miss Elizabeth, I fear I should never treat you as I have before. I was not always my best, you see."

Elizabeth recalled their first meeting at the assembly in Meryton and their subsequent trials. Still, the Mr. Darcy she'd come to know in the days after the accident seemed changed from the guarded gentleman that first night at the assembly. He was no longer ill at ease nor quiet for long stretches when in her company.

"The measure of a man is taken at different times in his life, Mr. Darcy. When he is young and without fear, one might say he will one day learn it. When he is older and has seen all there is to fear, one might say he is wise. But he is ever the same man, young or old, with dreams and hopes that never fade. I would know the whole of the man, good and bad, before I take his measure."

Mr. Darcy walked on considering her words. "Do you believe a man's character might change so and yet he remains the same?"

"I am not the girl I was ten years ago and yet I am in my mind. I know myself from then until now and that cannot change. But what can change is how that girl sees things now, ten years on, and how ten years from now I will see the woman I am today quite differently," Elizabeth's voice fell away and she sighed in contentment. She hoped Mr. Darcy might understand her meaning.

They walked in silence for a time behind the trio of couples before them and when they came upon a stone bench on the path, Mr. Darcy used his hand-kerchief to make a seat for his lady. Elizabeth sat, gratified at his chivalry and turned her gaze to him. "Will you sit with me?"

Mr. Darcy did not waste one moment in doing her bidding and happily sat closer to the lady than might have been proper. He cared not for there was no one about in the gardens. The other couples had carried on without them.

"What you said earlier, I do understand. The Fitzwilliam Darcy I was before my Father died and the man I am now are so very different and yet, the young man lives on inside still uneasy at times with all that he must do. The sister, the cousins, the family name, the estates, the tenants — all those responsibilities he would have surely failed if he had been fearful of his place in life."

It was Mr. Darcy's turn to fall silent and Elizabeth merely sat with him enjoying their easy camaraderie. When she thought of how much she'd learned of him in this quiet moment, a smile played across her lips to recall all their walks about Rosings before the accident when he'd kept his thoughts locked inside.

Fitzwilliam Darcy was changed and Elizabeth found she preferred this man to the one she'd met all those months ago in Meryton. And yet, even now, he was a mystery to her. To think that a man of his means, a man like Mr. Darcy, would have a moment's fear about who he was and the life he led had never occurred to Elizabeth Bennet.

But now, as she risked a glance his way she could see the years fall away and his profile as he glanced across the gardens seemed much younger in this light. What was it like to lose both your parents and become responsible for a younger sister and your family's wealth?

It could not have been easy and perhaps he had grown harder and less at ease among strangers as the years wore on. To hear gossip of your wealth and be chastised by those who'd never had even a tenth of the responsibility must surely have been a bitter pill.

Her heart was pierced for him and Elizabeth gulped back the tears that came. Mr. Darcy was a good man and she wanted to take him in her arms and say she was sorry for having thought any differently of him.

He seemed to sense her discomfort and mistook it for physical pain. Mr. Darcy stood abruptly and helped her to stand beside him. "Come, let me see you inside. There will be other days for walking. I would not see you in pain, Miss Elizabeth."

She began to protest, but her heart was full and her head had begun to hurt a little more as they sat. Elizabeth leaned against Mr. Darcy and began to walk with him again towards Rosings. He placed an arm about her shoulders to steady her and his face was a study in worry. "Miss Elizabeth, I could carry you inside if you like."

Elizabeth's reply of laughter pleased him, for he truly worried she might faint away here in the garden and then Dr. Green would say she must stay inside for a time. Mr. Darcy knew that was the worst medicine for his lady who loved to walk about everywhere she went.

He moved as though he meant to pick her up and Elizabeth stepped away. "Mr. Darcy, that will not be necessary. Only let me lean against you as we hasten back to the house."

Mr. Darcy honored her request but instead of placing her hand on his arm he placed his arm about her, drawing her closer to his side. He sheltered her there as they walked slowly back to the home.

Elizabeth breathed deeply to maintain her composure at this intimacy. The warmth of his body and the smell of his expensive cologne made her dream of dancing in his arms in a grand ballroom, loved and protected by a man she was coming to care for much more deeply than she thought possible.

When they gained the wide, stone steps of the home, Mr. Darcy reluctantly let her go but remained close to be certain she was steady on her feet.

Elizabeth knew her cheeks surely gave him a clue as to her feelings. The heat that rose there mimicked the leaping flame in her heart.

Glancing about, Mr. Darcy took her hand and placed it on his arm as though he hadn't just held her gently in his arms moments ago. Winking at her astonishment, Mr. Darcy cleared his throat and led Elizabeth slowly up the steps. "If anyone should complain, we would only say that you were feeling faint and I, being the gentleman I am, made certain you were returned quickly from the gardens."

Elizabeth walked haltingly with Mr. Darcy inside the front door of Rosings to help make his excuse true if the need arose.

The sound of laughter and excited chatter drifted inside as their companions came behind them. It seemed that Mr. Darcy and Miss Elizabeth were not the only couple of their party to have enjoyed the garden and a private conversation.

CHAPTER 18

Making their way to the parlor, Mr. Darcy was pleased to find the room empty and led Elizabeth to the sofa where she might recover from her walk. Turning as she was seated, Mr. Darcy welcomed the other couples into the room. "It appears we have the parlor to ourselves. Come Georgie and play for us if you will. I fear Anne and Miss Elizabeth require a brief rest before continuing upstairs."

Georgiana happily went to the piano forte and began perusing the many sheets of music her Aunt Catherine possessed. The woman claimed no skill with the playing of music and Georgie laughed to think of her words on the matter. She held that she should be a great proficient had she ever learned to play.

Selecting a slower melody, Miss Darcy soon lost

herself in her practice. Jane and Richard sat on the sofa across from Elizabeth and Anne. Dr. Green had led his walking partner to her seat next to Miss Elizabeth so that he might see to both his patients at once.

Mr. Darcy followed James Fitzwilliam to stand before the fireplace. His eyes never left Elizabeth Bennet's face and his cousin soon noticed the attraction. "I say Darcy, of all the young ladies you've met over the seasons in London I have never seen you so enchanted."

Darcy turned to assess his cousin's sincerity. "I do admire Miss Elizabeth for her wit and intellect. At present, she is only an acquaintance James."

James Fitzwilliam did not believe his cousin's words for a moment but before he might disagree, Georgiana ceased her playing and called to the assembled party. "With so many lovely ladies and gallant gentlemen present, I shall play a melody fit for dancing."

Mr. Darcy moved away from the mantel to find whether his lady might wish to dance. "Are you recovered from our walk Miss Elizabeth?"

"I am, Mr. Darcy but I would only watch for now as the others dance." Elizabeth did not wish for him to think she desired to dance for as she recalled, the man had never been fond of the diversion.

The Colonel stood and offered his hand to Jane and the doctor looked to Anne de Bourgh with much longing though he did not offer his hand to the lady.

Seeing that Miss Elizabeth would not dance, Mr. Darcy offered his hand to his cousin though he would have preferred to move about the room with the lady who held his heart. "Come Anne, I would be pleased to have you as my partner."

Moments after the dancing commenced, Lady Catherine and Lady Matlock entered the parlor. As they moved across the room, Lady Catherine gave a decided look of disapproval at the pairings.

Though her daughter Anne was dancing with Darcy, the sight of Miss Bennet with Colonel Fitzwilliam incensed the woman. She looked to Lady Matlock and pointed one bejeweled finger to the couple. "Would you see your second son married to a country lass without a fortune or connections?"

Lady Matlock did not wish to indulge the woman's foolish conjecture. "Richard shall marry well, 'tis only a dance and nothing more."

The two ladies chose seats away from Miss Elizabeth and watched as the couples finished their first dance. When Georgiana saw her aunts, she rose from her bench and went to greet them. Her grateful audience returned to their seats reluctantly for they had great fun before Lady Catherine arrived.

Now, Elizabeth and Jane sat together while the men stood alongside chairs or behind the sofa ready to listen intently to Lady Catherine's pronouncements. "Dr. Green, do you think it wise for Anne to undertake such a strenuous exercise as dancing after having walked about the garden?"

Dr. Green's expression was one of caution as he spoke, but he would not appease the woman. "Indeed, your ladyship. We shall not tire Miss Anne or Miss Elizabeth out with a dance or two. I find fresh air and the company of others to be a great help in this particular circumstance. One must not suffer loneliness when trying to recall lost memories. What if Miss Elizabeth does recall that night and there is no one about to offer companionship or solace? Such a terrible thing it would be!"

Mr. Darcy turned away to hide the grin the doctor's words brought and deemed the man higher in his estimation than before. He had known Dr. Green for many years, the man was his personal physician in London after all. That the doctor knew exactly the words to use when speaking with Lady Catherine in order to see that his authority was not questioned gave the master of Pemberley not a little satisfaction.

Lady Matlock, wishing to interrupt any further complaint from her hostess, looked to her son James and called him to her side. "Catherine, did you not say you must ride out with your steward and see to the spring planting? I know how dearly James wishes to accompany you today."

James Fitzwilliam bit back words of denial that would surely upset his mother and offered his arm to Lady Catherine. "Indeed, Mother is right as always. I shall be most grateful for such knowledge as you might impart, Aunt Catherine. Shall we await the steward in your study?"

Lady Catherine stood and took her nephew's arm with the feeling that she had been outmaneuvered by Lady Matlock. For what purpose, she was entirely uncertain. Before James could escort her to the parlor door, she turned to Anne and fixed her with an imperious gaze. "Do not allow yourself to become fatigued, Anne. I would think you ought to take tea and then retire to your rooms for a time."

Anne de Bourgh attempted to sound contrite. "Yes, Mother. It has been a most eventful morning."

Satisfied that her advice had been properly noted

and agreed upon, Lady Catherine allowed her nephew to lead her from the room.

Elizabeth gave a small sigh of relief as Miss Darcy rose and returned to the piano forte to play another lively tune for the young dancers.

This time, Mr. Darcy sought her as his partner while Dr. Green made known his intentions to Miss Anne. As before, Colonel Fitzwilliam led Jane to a spot beside the piano forte.

Lady Matlock smiled at the pairings not wishing to make comment upon which gentleman chose which lady.

She would not allow herself to think perhaps Catherine had been correct in her estimation of Richard and Miss Jane Bennet.

As the couples danced, she rose and pulled a cord near the fireplace to summon the butler. When the man arrived, she asked that tea be brought and returned to her seat.

Colonel Richard Fitzwilliam was her second son, her flesh and blood, and he would marry well when the time came. There was no harm in his enjoying the company of a lovely young gentlewoman during a holiday in Kent.

The music changed and the pairs began to dance

again and Margaret Fitzwilliam saw something breathtaking between her niece and the good doctor.

Anne was simply glowing with delight in the man's arms as he bent his head and whispered to her. He was quite handsome and taller than both her sons and Mr. Darcy. Had she not known he was a physician, Lady Matlock would have thought him the son of a peer by his grace and bearing.

She wondered at his family and thought perhaps he'd been disowned for choosing to practice medicine. One did not often see a common man in possession of such refinement nor the education required of a physician trained in London.

Her eyes turned to Darcy and Miss Elizabeth. On that score, she found she must agree with Catherine's wild ideas. It was plain to one and all that her nephew fancied the young lady.

Richard had assured her they were only acquaintances from Darcy's time in Hertfordshire with Mr. Bingley but now Margaret Fitzwilliam was not as certain of that fact as she had been before.

With a startling clarity, she believed one of the couples dancing before her was more than a little in love and perhaps not aware of it themselves. Looking again to her son and Miss Bennet, Lady Matlock pursed her lips as her eyes narrowed in her inspection of the pair.

Certainly the young lady was lovely, poised, and seemed to enjoy the company of her son as they moved through the steps of the dance. But then, any young lady would feel the same. Richard Fitzwilliam was a ruggedly handsome man with a fine, muscled physique from his years of soldiering. Any woman with a heartbeat would find herself happy to be at the center of his attention.

When Georgiana ended her melody, Lady Matlock called to them as the tea cart arrived. "Come sit with me and let us enjoy tea before the ladies return upstairs."

Now, instead of the men moving off to stand at a distance from the ladies, the couples sat beside one another as tea was poured. Lady Matlock chased away the feeling that matches had already been made and thought to keep her son occupied in the coming days so that he was not often in the company of Miss Bennet.

CHAPTER 19

THE NEXT MORNING, Jane walked briskly down the lane away from Rosings and toward the parsonage to visit Charlotte Collins. The parson's wife had been to Rosings to visit with Elizabeth several times but Jane wished for a quiet moment with woman to speak about Elizabeth's loss of memory.

She carried a small book with her and stopped at a particularly sunny spot in the road and seated herself upon a boulder that was situated just a few paces off the lane amid a riotous display of corn-flower blooms.

Opening her book to the place held by a green ribbon Elizabeth had given her from a shoppe in Hunsford, Jane admired her handiwork. She preferred to paint but sketching with graphite allowed her to draw anywhere she pleased and capture the moment before her.

Instead of beginning a sketch of the flowers that nodded in a soft breeze by her feet, Jane turned to the page that held an impressive likeness of Colonel Fitzwilliam. As birds flitted among the leaves above her head, she took up her graphite stick and began to soften the edges of his collar and look critically at her work.

Jane thought of their dances and conversation so that when a shadow fell across her book, she jumped up in surprise and dropped her graphite.

Colonel Fitzwilliam bent at once and retrieved the thing in its holder. "Please forgive me, Miss Bennet, I did not mean to startle you. It's just that I wondered what you were about. Your concentration on that book caused me to wander to your side. Might I have a look?"

Jane's heart raced and a lump rose in her throat. What would he think if he knew she had drawn his likeness? "Oh, I would not bore you with my amateur scratches, sir."

Holding the book tighter, Jane moved quickly to sidestep the man and lost her footing. Her arms flailed slightly for balance but Richard Fitzwilliam caught her easily in his arms.

The book lay open on ground between them but Jane was lost in his eyes. His face was mere inches from her own and the strength of his hands as he held her caused all rational thought to fly from her head.

"Miss Bennet," he whispered, his eyes traveling down to her lips that were now parted slightly in astonishment.

A rider on a horse galloped past on the road and Jane moved to free herself of her admirer's grasp. Her foot nudged the fallen book and she dropped her gaze. The page was open to the likeness of the man before her!

Colonel Fitzwilliam bent to retrieve the book before Jane might grab it and hide it again. He held it open before him and Jane wished she might disappear into thin air. "I have never seen such skill in all my life, Miss Bennet! I must say I appear handsomer to your eye than to my own mirror."

Jane reached for the book, her face hot and her heart still racing from the memory of his strong hands holding her steady a moment ago. "I cannot say why I was compelled to draw your likeness, sir. Only that your face holds such character that it was a pleasure to copy."

Colonel Fitzwilliam fought the urge to pull the

woman into his embrace and crush her lips with the urgent desire of a man who has by chance found his love returned. "I would not argue but this face is not so handsome as to draw the interest of every lady. Tell me, Miss Bennet, do you hold more than an artistic interest in your subject?"

Jane busied herself with placing her graphite in her skirt pocket. Stepping onto the lane to gain distance from the man who made her heart race like a thoroughbred, she spoke the words in her head before she might lose courage. "Perhaps, though a proper young lady would never admit such."

She turned away and forced her feet to continue on her path to the parsonage. Colonel Fitzwilliam chuckled to himself and strode to catch up with his lady.

Miss Bennet could not say that she preferred him without leaving herself a way to deny it in the case that he did not return her feelings. She was cautious and he admired that quality. He chose to discuss a safer topic in order to respect her wish to hide her feelings for him. "How is Miss Elizabeth? I believe she has feelings for my cousin but I would not think to ask her so."

Happy that the man had decided not to challenge her own feelings, Jane thought for a moment before revealing any knowledge of her sister's attraction to Mr. Darcy. "I would say that Lizzy admires Mr. Darcy far more now than she did when first they met. I had always thought him a gentleman but when a person is quiet and does not engage in idle chatter, people often mistakenly judge their motives."

Colonel Fitzwilliam agreed. "That is often the case. Darcy keeps his counsel unless he is in the company of family and dear friends. I would say he counts you and your sister among that number now."

Jane gave a smile that melted his already softened heart and Richard was certain his future now included marriage to the lovely lady before him. "Such a wonderful sentiment you share, Colonel Fitzwilliam. I believe that my sister now counts him as more than a mere acquaintance."

Richard noticed they were nearing the parsonage and did not wish their chance meeting to end. "I would be happy to walk with you back to Rosings if you wish."

Jane glanced to the front gate of the parsonage where her cousin and Charlotte made their home. "I would visit with Mrs. Collins for a time, first. I was hoping she might share what happened the day of Lizzy's accident so that I might be a better help to my sister. She is quite concerned that nothing of that day will reveal itself to her now."

Richard could not say what he wished about his knowledge of that day as he respected Darcy's privacy. "In that case, I shall wait near the bridge just ahead if you like. After you have visited Mrs. Collins, I will show you the path that leaves the lane there and brings us back to Rosings."

Jane waved as he walked on ahead of her and turned to lift the latch on the gate that would allow her entry to the stone path that led to her cousin's front door. If she doubted the man's feelings for her before, it was certainly clear now he wished to know her better. Her heart began its erratic pace again and she breathed deeply to regain her composure before sitting with Charlotte Collins.

❧

ELIZABETH LEFT Miss Anne's sitting room with her mind in a terrible mess. Dr. Green had sat with them after breakfast so that he might help her recall the memories that would not come to her of their own volition.

She had begged the man for any method that

might nudge her mind into recalling that day and he had reluctantly agreed. "Miss Elizabeth, I must warn you not to expect that my interference will necessarily produce any result that might cause you to remember much of that day."

Now as she descended the stairs to make her way to the library, Elizabeth thought of all that had transpired in Miss Anne's sitting room. Dr. Green had begun the conversation by having the young mistress speak of all she knew of that night.

Miss Anne closed her eyes and breathed deeply while Dr. Green spoke in a soothing tone of voice. He asked questions that required the young lady to elaborate on whatever revelation came about as she walked through that night in her mind.

It was clear Miss Anne had overheard a conversation that caused her to flee to the stables and have her gig made ready. She spoke of the chill air that night and riding by the parsonage to find Elizabeth and Mrs. Collins by the gate.

Elizabeth startled in her seat as she recalled lifting the latch of the gate and stepping onto the lane as Mr. Collins nodded to her. His words had come to her as she sat with Dr. Green and Miss Anne.

Go on then, Cousin Elizabeth, see her home. Lady Catherine shall be worried.

Shaking her head as she reached the bottom of the stairs, Elizabeth turned and walked past the parlor. The library was but a few steps further down the hallway and she hurried to seek the comfort of a good book there. Reading would settle her mind, she was sure of that much.

Upon entering the room, she glanced about not wishing to interrupt anyone who might be about. Finding the great room empty, she admired the rich, masculine decor and was happy to find a fire had been laid.

Not wanting to waste a moment, Elizabeth turned away from the fireplace and went to roam the shelves that housed more books than she'd ever seen gathered in one place.

While she chose between two novels, Mr. Darcy entered the room. He made his way to one of the two chairs before the fireplace and sat without having seen that his beloved was also in the room.

When Elizabeth could not choose between the two books, she kept them both and crossed the room to seat herself before the cheerful warmth of the fire. Before she might take a seat, she saw Mr. Darcy and halted her steps. "I am sorry, sir. I did not see you when I came in. I only came to find something to read."

Mr. Darcy stood abruptly and pleaded for her to remain. "Miss Elizabeth, please do not leave. This library is the perfect spot in all of Rosings to sit and read in peace."

Elizabeth gave the man a shy smile and followed as he led her to the chair next to his own. "Mr. Darcy, I would not stay and become a distraction if you wished to enjoy the library for yourself."

Mr. Darcy would not admit that her presence was indeed a great distraction but one that he welcomed more than she might think. "Miss Elizabeth, I had no plan to read when I entered the room. I would be quite happy to simply sit and warm myself before the fire while you read."

Placing her books on the table between them, Elizabeth gazed at Mr. Darcy as he settled against the dark upholstery of his chair. The silence between them was not uncomfortable and so she chose one of the books to begin.

As she read of a man who dared to profess his love to his lady, Elizabeth could feel Mr. Darcy's eyes upon her from time to time but would not lift her eyes from her book.

The words on the page pulled at her memory.

They were the fevered words of a man passionately in love. He was proposing marriage and his lady appeared quite shocked at the depth of emotion in his speech.

She closed the book and words came unbidden to her mind The voice that spoke them was most certainly that of Mr. Darcy.

In vain have I struggled. It will not do. My feelings will not be repressed. You must allow me to tell you how ardently I admire and love you.

Elizabeth bit her bottom lip to hold back a gasp but the whisper of a moan escaped and startled Mr. Darcy.

He stood quickly from his seat and came to kneel before her. "Miss Elizabeth, what is wrong?"

She could not think what to say so she merely covered her face with her hands and bowed her head. Shaken by this memory of Mr. Darcy professing to love her, Elizabeth whispered the words that would allow her the time to think on the memory. "I fear I am not well, Mr. Darcy. I must return upstairs to rest for a time."

Mr. Darcy helped her to stand and Elizabeth forced herself to drop her hands from her face. She glanced into his eyes and trembled at the worry she found residing there. Placing her hand on his arm,

Elizabeth lowered her head and spoke softly hoping to ease his mind. "Tis only a headache Mr. Darcy, I shall be well soon."

As he led her up the stairs to her room, Elizabeth recalled the crashing of the gig that night when the horse had been spooked by a fox that darted across the lane. She fought the urge to break into tears fearing Mr. Darcy would have the truth from her before she was able to sort it for herself.

CHAPTER 20

WHEN RICHARD FITZWILLIAM entered Rosings with Miss Bennet on his arm, Lady Matlock had been about to enter the parlor. Instead, her attention was drawn by the laughter of her son and the eldest Bennet sister.

"Richard, I meant to have you take me into Hunsford this afternoon. I promised Georgie I would look for some paper. Ever since her modiste gave her those drawings of dresses that will be made for her season, the girl has wished to make sketches of her own."

Jane left the mother and son to seek Elizabeth's company to discuss the conversation she'd had with Charlotte at the parsonage.

Richard watched Miss Bennet go with regret

before turning his attention to his mother. "I would be pleased to accompany you to Hunsford Mother, but first I require a cigar in the library. Miss Bennet and I had quite the walk this morning."

Lady Matlock was not pleased with this news. "Richard, you must not give Miss Bennet the wrong impression."

"Mother, it was only a walk back to Rosings. I came upon her in the lane quite by accident as she was set to visit Mrs. Collins. I assure you that Miss Bennet does not labor under the wrong impression." Richard kept the smile from his lips at this play on words. Jane Bennet had the exact impression he meant for her to have.

Instead of leaving him to enter the parlor, Lady Matlock followed her son as he strode to the library. "I would have a word with you, son."

Knowing his mother would not leave him in peace, Richard held the door as she entered. "Mother, I do intend to have a cigar but I shall wait until you've finished speaking your mind."

Lady Matlock did not like giving her son the upper hand but there was little else she might do.

Sitting with him as he selected his cigar, Lady Matlock spoke without preamble. "Entertaining

Miss Bennet leads me to believe you have forgotten your place, son. You are aware that your father and I expect you to marry from among the families of the Ton. There are any number of suitable young ladies with the connections to enhance the Fitzwilliam fortune."

"And large dowries as well. Am I correct?" Richard asked as a smile played on his lips. He raised the cigar to inhale the rich aroma while holding his mother's steely gaze.

"Naturally your father and I prefer a young lady of means as your brother shall have the lion's share of property and wealth being he is the first born son."

Colonel Fitzwilliam was not unaware of his parent's wishes. How might he ever be? It was a matter of fact that the earl wished him to leave his soldiering and settle as a country gentleman. There was a small country estate between Pemberley and the Matlock estate in Derbyshire that would fall to him upon his marriage.

"Mother, first and foremost, I am able to manage my own affairs. I am a grown man as you well know. Also, I am not accustomed to being dictated to, though my superiors do that quite well. But in matters that pertain to my future wife, let's just say that I shall marry for love and consider her dowry as a benefit and not an enticement."

Though he knew this would have the effect of keeping his mother longer in the library, Richard would not deceive her.

Lady Matlock tried another tack. "What you say is true, son. But you might reconsider marrying for love if you knew your father and I shall settle a handsome sum on your accounts in London once you choose a proper bride."

Startling his mother with a bellowing laugh, Richard reached for the matches in the drawer of the humidor. "Oh Mother, you do always have a way of making your point abundantly clear. Let us not argue the matter further for there is not a way that you might purchase my heart, but I promise to give consideration to all that you have said here today."

Lady Matlock rose from her seat as Richard struck the match and lifted it to his cigar. Perhaps if she could make no impression upon her headstrong son she might have better luck with Miss Bennet.

Lady Catherine sat behind her ornate desk in her study with Dr. Green before her. The man was certain this was no casual meeting he'd been summoned to attend.

"I would have a full report on the health of my daughter, doctor."

Dr. Green tried to hide his relief at her words. He suspected she might have seen through his professional demeanor to the man beneath that had fallen in love with her daughter.

He relaxed his long frame into the chair before her desk and settled his hands on the richly, upholstered arms. Once, many years ago, he sat in his father's study listening as the old man spoke of his expectations for his second son. Though he did not come from a titled family, Dr. Green's forebears were landed gentry and his father's expectations were as ambitious as any titled family.

Now, as he glanced about the room, he found himself wondering how his life might have been had he listened to his father. He would never have met Anne de Bourgh and that fact alone was quite enough to make him happy with his choice to become a physician.

Though he did not hold near the wealth of Miss

Anne's family, he was quite capable of keeping a wife and a home without much concern. He did not think for a moment Lady Catherine would agree, however.

His father had died several years ago and his eldest brother had been far more accepting of Harry Green's choices in life. He had a lovely townhouse in London and a healthy five thousand pounds per annum his brother had settled on him. But having been at Rosings for nearly a week, Dr. Green knew his townhouse in London would be considered a step down in society for Miss Anne de Bourgh.

Pushing these thoughts aside, he addressed the lady before him in his most professional tone. "Your ladyship, your daughter is recovering quite nicely and I am pleased to say she has steadily regained her strength and appears to benefit from the presence of so many companions."

Lady Catherine did not care in the least what the man thought of the guests currently residing under her roof. "Be that as it may, I am confident that soon the Bennet sisters may leave us and return to Mr. Collins and his wife at the parsonage."

Dr. Green hated to be disagreeable, especially with the mother of the lady he planned to make his wife, but there was no need for Miss Elizabeth to leave Rosings. "I would advise against such a move at the moment, your ladyship. Miss Elizabeth appears to be well, though it may be that her sister's arrival has given her spirits a lift, but my main concern is for Miss Anne. She has an attachment for Miss Elizabeth and I fear parting them would set both back in their recovery. Certainly you would not wish for such a thing?"

Watching the lady's expression, Dr. Green was certain she did indeed want Elizabeth Bennet gone from her home no matter the cost. When she spoke, he was not prepared for her declaration. Certainly not where Miss Anne de Bourgh was concerned.

"Dr. Green, I must be frank. Elizabeth Bennet is a great threat to the future happiness of my daughter. Mr. Darcy is to marry my Anne and I fear Miss Elizabeth harbors thoughts to the contrary. So you see, I would be most grateful were you to say she might leave Rosings. Most grateful."

Lady Catherine raised her brow on the last words and Dr. Green knew full well she meant to provide him with a tidy sum if he did exactly as she requested.

The news of the match between Mr. Darcy and his Anne shook the doctor to his core but he was not willing to give up his dream so easily and certainly not for any sum of money. "Your ladyship, it is a highly unusual favor you ask of me and while I understand your concern, I could not possibly betray my training nor my profession by putting my patients at risk for any reason."

The woman was incensed and stood abruptly from her seat. "Perhaps I shall have need to find another physician from London who might be willing to do as I ask. You may go Dr. Green but do not be surprised to find yourself replaced in the coming days."

Dr. Green stood and gave a small bow to the mistress of Rosings. He dared not speak again on the matter but his mind was quickly working to form a plan before he found himself cast out of Rosings and away from Anne de Bourgh.

Thinking his only recourse was to admit his feelings for the lady and seek her hand, Dr. Green left the study and found himself racing up the stairs two at a time with his aim of finding Anne de Bourgh and making his desires known.

IN HER ROOMS, Anne sat with her cousin and

thought of her earlier meeting with Dr. Green and Miss Elizabeth. She had revealed as much about the night of the accident as possible without speaking of her cousin's failed proposal. She wondered if Miss Elizabeth had managed to recall anything of that night after she'd left them to go down to the library.

Turning to her cousin, Anne thought to find if the improvement in her own health was as obvious to others as it was to herself. "Georgie, do you think I am better than you've ever seen me before?"

Georgiana Darcy looked at her cousin and touched her face gently. "You are, Anne! I am surprised each time Dr. Green says that we must let you rest. All the times before, whenever William and I would come, you never seemed as happy as you are now. It does not make sense, I suppose, for you were injured. It must be that Dr. Green is such a wonderful physician."

Anne sighed at her cousin's mention of the man who was stealing her heart. It was because of his presence, and not because of his medical expertise, that she was happier and healthier. She longed to do exactly as he instructed but there was so much more than that.

Harry Green, Anne smiled to herself to think of the conversation in the garden that led to him to reveal his Christian name, was the epitome of the man of her dreams. The one she'd conjured from the novels she hid and Georgie's letters full of gossip about the balls and parties she'd gleaned from her brother since Georgie was much too young to attend such events herself.

In her dreams, Anne had danced with him in the ballroom of Rosings. He had kissed her softly and spoke of his undying love. There was a future with Harry Green that she looked forward to each night as she rested her head on her pillows.

Anne noticed the color returning to her cheeks and the sparkle in her eyes when she sat before the mirror of her dressing table and knew without a doubt that the presence of Dr. Harry Green was the reason for the miraculous change.

Now, as she sat listening patiently to Georgiana's latest bit of gossip gleaned from the Bingley sisters in London, Anne de Bourgh thought of the wish that had come to her that morning as her maid brushed her hair and arranged it artfully with jewel encrusted combs.

In her mind, she wished for Harry to make a proposal to her, had even dreamed it before waking that morning but when she sat before the dressing table, it was another proposal that tickled at her memory.

It was to do with her cousin Darcy and Miss Elizabeth and their postponed happiness. She'd spoken to her friend about Darcy whenever they were alone together and Miss Elizabeth had said he was very different now than when they'd first met.

Anne was drawn back to the conversation as Georgiana said something about Charles Bingley and Jane Bennet. "To think she may have ended up as Mrs. Bingley seems wrong when I see her with Richard, don't you agree?"

Sighing, Anne took her cousin's hand. "It seems that love will find a way, Georgie, no matter how we might try and bend it to our own desires."

Georgiana gave the doe eyed expression so many young ladies wore when speaking of love. "I hope that I might find a handsome husband to love me one day. Maybe when my season comes? Oh, you have not seen the drawings from my modiste in London! Let me get them and we can decide which you like best. Brother has said I must have several dresses made just for my season."

As Georgiana rose and kissed her forehead, Anne remained silent as she thought of Georgie as a married woman. Her cousin quit the room and closed the door softly behind her. Anne allowed her mind to return to Darcy and Miss Elizabeth.

The thought that Miss Elizabeth might recall her refusal of Darcy's proposal before she remembered that she wished to apologize to the man gave Anne pause. Perhaps she ought to speak privately with her friend on the matter?

Before she could plot further, a knock came upon her sitting room door. Her voice was timid when she called out for her guest to enter but when the door opened and Harry Green appeared, she spoke clearly. "Oh Dr. Green, do come in. I was just thinking of our meeting with Miss Elizabeth this morning."

Dr. Green hurried to his lady and sat, taking her small hands in his large, warm grasp. At once, Anne felt all worry leave her and moved closer to him on the sofa.

"Would you care to share your thoughts?" he asked, his eyes conveying his concern.

Noticing that her heart was beating much faster after his arrival, Anne wished she had one of her many fans at hand. "There was a good reason for my leaving Rosings that evening. I would do it again even knowing the outcome though I would never say so to Mother."

Dr. Green smiled at his lovely lady. She was all that was good and kind, such a stark contrast to Lady Catherine. "I must say although it pains me deeply that you were frightened and hurt in that accident, it has brought me here to your side and I cannot think of my life without you now."

Anne was not prepared for such strong emotion from the man of her dreams. Happy tears gathered in her eyes and she fought to keep them from clouding her vision. She wished to always remember the sincere expression of devotion on Harry's face as he awaited her reply to his sudden passionate outburst.

She could not believe the words he had spoken, not until he pulled her into his arms and whispered more urgently of his feelings. "Oh Anne, my Anne, I have loved you since the moment I saw you. I know it is not the thing a man like myself ought to hope for, and not after so brief an acquaintance, but I dearly wish for you to be my wife."

The happy tears fell then, for how else might a sheltered young lady feel to suddenly have her dreams come true?

Allowing Harry to take her face in his hands, Anne watched intently as he moved to press his lips to hers. It was a wholly thrilling prospect and nothing she had ever read in her novels could have prepared her for this moment.

After his gentle kiss, Anne thought to be certain of his feelings. "Harry, are you sure? You cannot know the sickly girl I was before you came as I have not always been well. I may never bear children…"

Her voice faltered and Anne cast her eyes down to hide her shame at admitting such to a man. She'd thought the words many times in the privacy of her rooms but speaking them aloud was far worse than she expected.

Harry squeezed her hands with the greatest of care and Anne lifted her eyes to meet his gaze. He spoke the words she longed to hear. "I know not what future lies ahead but I would share it without a care for whether we are blessed with offspring. If it is your wish to one day become a mother, why there are any number of physicians in London who might advise us on the matter."

Her concerns in that quarter satisfied, Anne took up the objection her mother would surely make. "The only other obstacle would be my mother's idea of who I ought to marry."

Dr. Green gave a laugh at this. Lady Catherine's revelation of her hopes for Mr. Darcy and Anne had been the impetus that drove him to confess himself to her daughter so soon. "I am aware that she believes you ought to marry Mr. Darcy, in fact it was that very admission on her part that brought me to your rooms to make my audacious claim."

Anne's blue eyes twinkled with mirth. "Mother often is her own worst enemy but I am pleased her machinations drove you into my arms, Harry. For my part, you must know that I accept your suit. I will become Anne Green but first I have a duty to my cousin. You see, there is a lady he loves and wishes to marry. I must see them engaged before we might have our wedding. Our own engagement shall remain a secret for now if you do not mind."

Harry Green delighted in the sparkle in his beloved's eyes. She was a most precious jewel hidden within this grand estate and he the most fortunate man to have found her and won her heart. "I do not mind and I will not press for details about your cousin's situation my dear, but I do advise that you not go dashing off again in a gig in order to accomplish your goal. Do I have your word?"

Anne gazed into the warm, gray eyes of her beloved and made a solemn vow. "I promise to seek your counsel before acting in a manner that could end badly for all involved."

It was enough for Harry Green. He would never

seek to censor the woman he loved, only to protect her and aid her whenever he might. He knew in his heart she'd suffered much too long under strictures that had left her believing she would never have a life beyond Rosings.

CHAPTER 21

JANE KNOCKED upon Elizabeth's door and entered after waiting a moment. Elizabeth was sitting by the only window in the room and Jane considered leaving since her presence had not been noted.

Instead, she crossed the room and took a seat beside her sister. Elizabeth turned her face and Jane was shocked to find she had been crying. "Oh Lizzy, what has happened? Are you in pain? I will go and get Dr. Green!"

Elizabeth reached out and took Jane's hand. "Do not bother Dr. Green. It is only that I remember some of that day. Oh, Jane, Mr. Darcy admitted that he loved me!"

Jane's expression became one of excitement but she attempted to remain calm. Until her sister's memory of the man's proposal returned, Jane was unsure how much of that knowledge to share. Charlotte had told her of the proposal and her sister's refusal during her visit earlier in the day. "Oh Lizzy, do you remember more of that day or the accident?"

Elizabeth stood and crossed the room to splash her face with cool water from the basin on her washstand. Turning to Jane, she moved to the bed and twisted her hands before sitting on the edge in agitation. "I remember the fox that darted across the road and the horse rearing up, it was so terrible Jane. I tried to hold onto Miss Anne and keep her from being thrown to the road."

Joining her sister on the bed, Jane placed an arm around her trembling form. "Oh, I know it must have been terrible my dear. You did all you could to help her that night and became the one who was the most injured."

Before she might guard her expression, Elizabeth allowed the tears to fall that she'd hidden earlier from Mr. Darcy. "I have tried again and again since this morning to remember all that Mr. Darcy said but my mind is a locked door and I cannot find the key."

Jane smoothed Elizabeth's hair and retrieved a handkerchief from her skirt pocket. "There now, my sweet Lizzy, go on and have a good cry. You have had such trials at Kent."

Elizabeth leaned into her sister and sobbed over her lost memories. Surely they would come again? When she was done, Jane helped her to the basin once more and washed her tear-stained face.

Guiding her sister to the dressing table, Jane began to unpin her hair. "Mr. Darcy has never been a man of sweet words and poetic speech. What exactly did he say?"

Elizabeth delighted in the feel of Jane's fingers in her hair and closed her eyes to think of the words that had haunted her ever since she left the library with Mr. Darcy.

Repeating the words as she recalled them, Elizabeth kept her voice low. "In vain have I struggled. It will not do. My feelings will not be repressed. You must allow me to tell you how ardently I admire and love you."

Elizabeth sighed before realizing how romantic it all must sound. Jane laughed gently and gathered the weight of her sister's curls to smooth the strands before she began to pin them in place again. "How utterly perfect those words seem! Too perfect for Mr. Darcy, for he has never been a man of romantic words. I imagine it was difficult for him to speak so of his emotions, Lizzy."

Elizabeth allowed the joy at knowing Mr. Darcy

loved her to show upon her face. "My heart believes now that he is the man I always wanted him to be, Jane. He is so very different in many ways. There are things I never knew of him but hearing from Miss Anne and Miss Darcy of his kindness and knowing he brought his physician here to see that I was recovered, I fear I misjudged him before. Do you think he loves me still?"

"I do, Lizzy. He has shown it throughout the time I have been at Rosings. He must think that if he humbles himself and makes you see the man he truly is, there may be a happy future for the two of you."

Elizabeth hugged her favorite sister tightly. "I find myself wishing for such, Jane!"

Once Elizabeth released her, Jane began to fuss over her sister's dress. Catching her Jane's hands to still them from their task, Elizabeth broached the subject of Colonel Fitzwilliam. "And where were you this morning, dear sister? I detected a hint of cologne on your sleeve earlier as you brushed my hair and I believe I know which gentleman wears that particular scent."

Jane's face immediately turned a bright pink. "I met the Colonel on my walk this morning. He saw the drawing of his likeness in my book, Lizzy. I think he must know I hold feelings for him. I cannot believe I have fallen in love so soon! I promised myself I would go slow this time."

Elizabeth squeezed Jane's hands and tried to contain her excitement. "Oh, Jane! There is no choice when it comes to love. You cannot choose it like a ribbon or a pretty bolt of silk. Would waiting to love him make a difference?"

Jane swiped at the happy tears her sister's support had brought. "I cannot wait to love him, Lizzy, I already do! But what will his family think?"

"They will think the same no matter the length of your acquaintance, I fear. Lady Matlock surely expects he will marry as well as his brother. There is nothing either of us might do to change who we are, Jane. I do not think the Colonel will stop loving you because of objections from his family."

Jane hugged Elizabeth tightly and allowed herself to simply hope that her love for Richard Fitzwilliam would be enough in the end.

ॐ

LATER THAT SAME evening in the parlor, Anne de Bourgh sat beside her mother studiously ignoring Dr. Green while attempting to conceal her excitement. If she looked at him, she was certain she might admit their love for one another to all present. She was not prepared when her mother spoke of hiring another physician.

Elizabeth and Jane were present along with Lady Matlock and Miss Darcy but the men sat across the room awaiting the arrival of the tea cart.

As a maid entered pushing the much awaited repast, Lady Catherine spoke of her plans as Mr. Darcy and the men moved across the room to join the ladies. "Dr. Green and I had quite the conversation earlier in my study and I believe it is time to seek the opinion of another physician. I am not of the mind that his care has made any difference for my Anne."

Mr. Darcy began to address his aunt but Anne spoke up instead. "Mother, I cannot understand how it is that you of all people do not see the color in my cheeks nor notice the improvement in my health since Dr. Green arrived. I am able to think of the accident without fear now. You will not force him from Rosings. If you do, I shall follow him to London and seek his care there."

Lady Catherine turned on her only child and cut her to the quick. "You will do no such thing, foolish girl! I am your mother, the one who has seen to your care for many years. Where might you stay in London? You have only the means I provide and I will not allow such disobedience."

Mr. Darcy would not listen to another word against Anne or Dr. Green. Though he knew his aunt was difficult at best, she had gone too far in her abuse of the young lady in the presence of her assembled guests. "Aunt Catherine, I agree with Anne. If you send Dr. Green away I shall see her to London myself. She is welcome to stay at Darcy House as long as she wishes. You seem to forget that she is no longer a child and you cannot bend her to your will."

The Bennet sisters were deeply uncomfortable at the airing of a family disagreement and stood to leave. Dr. Green, feeling much the same, offered an arm to each sister and quit the parlor without hesitation.

Georgiana Darcy looked to her brother and at the nod of his head, quit the parlor with her cousins James and Richard. Soon, there was only Lady Matlock and Mr. Darcy left to defend poor Anne against her mother.

"Darcy, you have no authority here! You are exactly like your mother, much too kind, and it causes me great pain. You would shirk your responsibility to Anne for that Bennet girl and see your cousin married to her sister! I will not stand for such scandalous behavior at Rosings."

Lady Matlock was in agreement with Lady Catherine in so far as the presence of her family at Rosings. "Darcy, I would agree with Catherine. I do not wish to linger a moment longer and have my sons and nieces questioned at every turn when they have done nothing to warrant such censure."

Lady Catherine stood and glared at her brother's wife. The woman had never truly respected her and kept her brother and nephews far from Rosings. "I shall call for the carriages to be brought around, Margaret."

Mr. Darcy stepped between the ladies and held up his hands. His aunt's mention of his mother angered him greatly but he had not the luxury of drawing out the argument with his aunt for the sake of defending his mother. It was an oft repeated barb the mistress of Rosings used on him and he chose to leave it.

He did not wish to leave without securing Miss Elizabeth's hand. It seemed the situation in Kent was quickly unraveling and he did not wish to be on the losing end.

"Aunt Catherine, I know you do not want Anne to leave with us and she will, I assure you. Anne said she is able to think of that evening without fear though I am certain you missed that in your eagerness to dismiss Dr. Green. If the man's methods have helped her, then you must allow him to stay for the remainder of his fortnight. Perhaps by then, Anne will be completely recovered and he may return to London."

Lady Catherine eyed the parlor door for a split second before turning to her nephew. "I will endure his presence, and that of the Bennet sisters for one more week Darcy. After that, they must make other plans and leave Rosings never to return."

Leaving her nephew and Lady Matlock to stare after her, Lady Catherine turned to her daughter. "I would speak with you in private. Come along to my study, Anne."

Glancing to Darcy and her Aunt Margaret for a moment, Anne obeyed her mother.

Once they had left the parlor, Lady Catherine began to berate the remainder of her guests who had remained in the entryway of Rosings instead of dispersing throughout the house. She whirled on Colonel Fitzwilliam and sneered at him as she took her daughter by the arm. "You may have the parlor, the lot of you, for I would not dream of abiding such foolishness again today."

Richard bit his tongue to hold back the words he wished to say. *Bitter old biddy* his mind supplied. He exerted his will not to chuckle at his internal voice as his aunt turned and steered Anne to her study.

The Bennet sisters moved toward the stairs as one but Colonel Fitzwilliam held out an arm. "Miss Bennet, would you care to join me for tea? It appears the parlor is now free of embarrassing conversation."

Jane smiled and took his arm. "Do you think your mother would mind?"

Richard Fitzwilliam was not the least concerned with what his mother might think. "Mother is likely as embarrassed as the rest of us. Let us go in and attempt to forget these unhappy moments."

Dr. Green offered his arm to Elizabeth though his gaze wandered in the direction his beloved had gone with her mother. Elizabeth noted the look of concern on the man's face and thought to speak to Anne about her doctor later that evening. James and Miss Darcy followed behind and soon the party was reassembled in the parlor.

Mr. Darcy was pleased to see the return of the group and called for the maid who had left the room when the argument began. "Let us speak of happier things, shall we? Dr. Green, thank you for your patience. I am pleased with the progress Anne and Miss Elizabeth have made under your care."

Dr. Green shrugged his shoulders. "I want to thank you sir for your kind words earlier. I would hate to leave Miss Anne and Miss Elizabeth now. Though your cousin is doing well, I cannot see her left here alone just yet."

Elizabeth accepted her tea and glanced at Dr. Green. She had not found the time to speak with him about her memory of that day and now she doubted herself and wondered if her recollection had been correct.

Glancing about the room, she wished she might slip away for a moment to sort her worries. Placing her cup on the table before her, Elizabeth stood and excused herself. Mr. Darcy watched as she crossed the room to stand near the French doors that led to a small terrace overlooking a corner of the gardens.

As she pushed open one door slightly, he stood and walked to the fireplace to pretend interest at the conversation between his cousin James and Dr. Green. After a moment, Mr. Darcy moved across the room to peer through the French doors.

He halted before joining her wondering if he ought to return to the conversations in the parlor. She stood with one hand on the stone railing before her while the other was placed against her forehead. Thinking she might be in pain, he forgot his reticence and moved swiftly to her side.

"Miss Elizabeth," he said, his voice deep and low in order not to startle her.

Elizabeth turned and dropped the hand from her forehead. "Mr. Darcy, I did not mean to cause concern. I have had some memories of that night return to me today and I am not sure what is true and what is not."

Her eyes shone with unshed tears and Mr. Darcy moved closer to her. He struggled not to take her in his arms. He recalled the advice of Dr. Green not to question her but surely if he only offered some information it might ease her concerns? But it might also cause her to remember his proposal. Knowing the risk of revealing his visit, Mr. Darcy pushed away thoughts of losing Miss Elizabeth.

"Perhaps if I shared some part of that day, some small thing, it might be of assistance? I should not tell you this, and Dr. Green may disapprove, but I cannot see you like this and not take pity."

Elizabeth waited as he gathered his courage.

"I came to the parsonage that afternoon to speak with you on a matter of great importance. I fear my words were inadequate, perhaps even offensive. It was never my intent to cause you a moment's discomfort."

Mr. Darcy bit his tongue to keep from revealing more of the matter and instead moved closer to the lovely lady whose eyes now held questions he could not answer. Elizabeth turned away to catch her breath. Her memory had been true, Mr. Darcy had said he loved her!

She recalled perfectly well their disagreements in Hertfordshire that had set her against him. In the time since her accident he had been kinder and eager for her company, the man she'd always hoped he might be beneath the thorny surface.

The proud and haughty man was gone and in his place was a gentleman she had come to admire. The way he behaved with his sister and Miss Anne, his defense of those he loved, his trust in Dr. Green, the way he risked losing her now by admitting his folly, all of it was a revelation to Elizabeth.

Whatever he had said to her on his visit to the parsonage that day, it mattered not. Turning to gaze into his eyes, Elizabeth gathered her thoughts. "Mr. Darcy, I thank you for your kindness. You did not need to share with me a moment you have come to regret so that I might be at ease. There has been enough discord between us. Perhaps we ought to go forward forgiving one another of our trespasses?"

The light in Mr. Darcy's eyes gave her much hope and Elizabeth wanted to tell him all that she knew and all that he'd become to her in the past days. Before she might speak, Richard appeared and waggled his eyebrows at the couple. "Mother is convinced that if we leave the two of you out here alone another moment there shall be terrible consequences."

Mr. Darcy stepped away from Elizabeth as her sister appeared behind his cousin. He could hear the melodic strains of a lively tune in the parlor and knew his sister was bound to ask them all to dance again while she played.

Offering his arm to Miss Elizabeth, he saw that she had been staring at him as Richard and her sister turned and left them on the terrace. If his proposal had been successful, he could have swept her into his arms in that moment and kissed her with all the love in his heart. As it stood, he did not know when she might recall his proposal and refuse him again.

CHAPTER 22

L ADY C ATHERINE WAITED as her daughter took the chair Dr. Green had sat in a few hours prior. There was much subterfuge afoot at Rosings and she meant to have answers from her only child.

Without wasting another moment, Lady Catherine spoke as Anne avoided her gaze. "I wish to know why you went out in your gig that night. I have been patient, Anne, but I must know now."

Anne thought of what she might say to her mother that would not involve the telling of a lie. She would not speak of Darcy's proposal to Miss Elizabeth. "I only wished to be out in the countryside. There was no one about and so I thought to make a quick turn about the grounds and return home. I saw Miss Elizabeth at the parsonage as I was passing and asked her to join me."

Lady Catherine could not hide her agitation. She stood abruptly and leaned across her desk in an intimidating display of anger. "Listen to me, Anne. The Bennet sisters have their sights set on your cousins. Lady Matlock pretends not to see it but I most certainly do. The shades of Pemberley shall not be thus polluted. Why have you not encouraged Darcy's attentions so those wretched Bennet sisters might see their scheme is in vain?"

Anne thought of Dr. Green's visit to her sitting room to calm herself in the face of her mother's tirade. It would be foolish for her to admit to their secret courtship and the doctor's proposal with her mother already suspicious of every young person at Rosings save her cousins, Georgiana and James.

Instead, she relied upon her tried and true excuses when it came to the topic of one day becoming the wife of her cousin Darcy. "Mother, surely you know Fitzwilliam and I shall never wed. He wishes to have heirs for Pemberley and I am not so well as to supply that need. Surely, after all this time without a proposal from him, you might see you are wrong on the matter?"

"I do not care whether Darcy wishes to marry you, Anne. It is his duty to this family! I am certain that Georgiana, once married, will do a fine job of supplying heirs for Darcy's consideration. It is not unheard of you know."

Wishing her mother would relent but knowing it was an impossible dream, Anne rose slowly from her chair. "I would return to the parlor and see to our guests. Your outburst has left them all most uncomfortable."

Lady Catherine waved her daughter away knowing there was little else to be said to impress upon the foolish girl the importance of keeping Rosings in the family.

The worst outcome would be if she died without having managed to force a marriage between Darcy and her only child. "Oh yes, worry for the things that matter the least Anne. That is your way. While you are perfectly happy to waste your time, you might remember that my concern lies with Rosings and securing it for future generations of this family."

Anne hid the satisfied smile that crept across her lips as she turned to quit the study. She had kept the important news of the secret proposals of Dr. Green and her cousin Darcy from her mother. There was no concern on her part for Rosings. Future generations of her family would keep the estate through her marriage to Harry Green.

Now, as she returned to the parlor, the sound of

Georgiana's accomplished hand at the piano forte caused her to quicken her steps. She wished to dance with the man who would be her husband.

Thinking on how she might encourage Miss Elizabeth to recall that night in her gig, Anne de Bourgh entered the parlor happier than she could ever remember being in all her years at Rosings.

Her cousins were dancing with the Bennet sisters and she glanced to her aunt, Lady Matlock. She was engaged in conversation with James but eyed the dancing couples from time to time.

Across the way, Harry Green saw his beloved enter the room and attempted to school his expression. His face, whenever he saw her now, was a mix of emotions that were not easily concealed.

Anne waited for him, her own expression unguarded. It was so seldom she experienced true happiness that to hide it seemed an impossible feat. When he asked her to dance, her eyes lingered on his lips recalling the kiss they had shared in her sitting room.

Taking his hand and following him to join the other two couples, Anne lost herself in the joy of the moment. She would not think of the accident nor of Darcy's failed proposal until later when she was alone in her rooms. For now, she danced the way she might have danced had she been allowed her season in London. Harry was all that she might have dreamed for herself and her mother's wishes no longer mattered.

Elizabeth whispered to Mr. Darcy as she watched Dr. Green and Anne de Bourgh move past them. "Forgive me if my words are without merit, but don't you think Miss Anne is much happier now? Before, when I first came to Kent, there was a wistful sadness to the lady, a melancholy that seemed out of place for one so young and beautiful."

Mr. Darcy followed Elizabeth's gaze as she turned again to watch the young mistress and her physician. "Aunt Catherine has kept her hidden away for so many years. I expect his attentions have given her a taste of what her life might have been had she been brought to London for her season. I do admire the man. I have never seen my cousin as lively and I see it has everything to do with his presence."

As the music ended, Elizabeth was reluctant to leave Mr. Darcy but Lady Matlock had called Miss Darcy to her side. Elizabeth joined Jane on the sofa while Darcy called the gentlemen to his side. "While I would dearly love to stay and dance with each lady present in her turn, you are all aware I am not a great fan of the exercise. Gentlemen, would you care to join me in the library instead?"

Colonel Fitzwilliam and the doctor seemed hesitant but James rose swiftly from the seat beside his mother to join Mr. Darcy. "Come Richard, I believe Darcy has some choice cigars for us that he brought from Pemberley. Aunt Catherine's supply is sufficient but not as top notch as what the master of Pemberley might supply."

Looking to Jane and leaving her with a smile that brought a pretty pink stain to her cheeks, Richard drew the doctor along with him as he quit the room. "There's little that might lure me from the company of beautiful ladies but a cigar from Darcy's reserves is almost worth the sacrifice."

Dr. Green glanced over his shoulder at his Anne, knowing he must remain composed when in the company of her family. He thought he might speak with Darcy in the library if he found a moment alone with the man to ease his conscience of the burden of his secret with Miss de Bourgh.

He did not care for the appearance of impropriety where she was concerned. At least if he spoke with Darcy, his mind would be clear when it came time to make their announcement to the family.

Once the men were gone, Lady Matlock turned

to the remaining ladies. Instead of avoiding the topics raised by their host, she decided to handle the matter as delicately as possible. "I feel I must make an apology for Catherine's display. It is not to be borne though this is her home and she may speak as she pleases. Were we at Matlock House in London or our estate in Derbyshire, well, things are done quite differently."

The Bennet sisters looked to one another for support and Elizabeth spoke at last. "Your ladyship, perhaps Lady Catherine is simply overwhelmed by the accident and is not herself? Miss Anne is her only child so it is understandable if that is indeed the case."

Lady Matlock took the measure of Elizabeth Bennet then, for the young lady was judicious not to speak ill of her host. The mention of the accident caused her to remember that her niece could speak of the event without alarm. "Anne, you said earlier that the memory of the accident no longer overwhelms you. Why were you out so late alone?"

Having just brushed over the particulars of the accident with her mother, Anne de Bourgh did not hesitate to say the same as Lady Matlock waited expectantly. "Aunt Margaret, I fear it is not as exciting as Mother might have hoped. I recall leaving

Rosings in my gig and driving down the lane that leads to the parsonage. It was evening and I remember being cold in spite of my heavy dress. I only wanted to take a turn about the grounds and came upon Miss Elizabeth at the parsonage."

Miss Darcy turned to Elizabeth. "Have you any recollection of that night?"

Elizabeth attempted to hide her surprise at this question. She did not wish to speak of Mr. Darcy's proposal to all assembled, not before she had spoken to him on the matter. "I wish that I might Miss Darcy, but as yet I have not."

Miss Darcy seemed saddened but turned to Jane and spoke of her wish to continue their friendship in London. "When we have all returned to Town, I would dearly love to offer an invitation for tea."

Jane noticed Lady Matlock's slight gasp that was covered quickly by the woman's hand as she turned her head and gave a small cough. She knew the woman might not wish to renew their acquaintance in Town, however she would not deny her young friend. "I would be thrilled to visit you, Miss Darcy. Elizabeth and I shall be in Town as our relatives travel to the Lake district come the summer."

Seizing upon these words, Lady Matlock wished to know more about the relations the

Bennet sisters had in Town. When she had sent a footman to Cheapside with an express for Miss Bennet she had not thought of the woman's connections so great was her worry for Anne's condition. "In our haste to travel to Kent, I did not make their acquaintance. What does your uncle do in Town?"

Jane glanced to Elizabeth before answering the lady. Certainly once she knew of their uncle's living in trade the invitation to tea might not be forthcoming. "Uncle Edward is in trade and their townhouse is situated close to his warehouses there."

Lady Matlock kept her expression serene at this information. Miss Bennet was indeed a beautiful young lady who was the daughter of a gentleman but relatives in trade disqualified her from consideration as a daughter-in-law in Margaret Fitzwilliam's mind.

Miss Darcy spoke up then. "Aunt Margaret, you must help me to host a proper tea. Having the Bennet sisters as guests until we depart for Pemberley will be wonderful experience for the day I may be the mistress of an estate."

The lady smiled at her niece knowing the girl only wished to deepen her acquaintance with the Bennet sisters, especially Miss Jane Bennet. She could not have known that her dearest aunt would not wish to encourage a relationship between the eldest Bennet sister and her second son.

"What a capital idea, Georgie! It would be lovely to host them in the salon of Darcy House. 'Tis much brighter and more cheerful than my parlor in Town."

At this, Lady Matlock rose from her seat to leave the young ladies to their own conversation. She did not wish to offer support for Catherine's outburst but an afternoon spent watching her son dance with Miss Bennet and the invitation from her niece to the sisters left her little choice. The sooner the Bennets were returned to the welcoming arms of their cousin and Mrs. Collins, the better for all.

CHAPTER 23

IN THE LIBRARY, Harry Green sat enjoying one of the fine cigars Mr. Darcy had his valet bring down after the men had left the ladies in the parlor.

The Fitzwilliam brothers were well into a rousing game of chess, insults and boasts flying between them, when he thought to speak with Mr. Darcy regarding his intentions.

Choosing his words with care, Harry Green decided there would be no better time than the present. "Mr. Darcy, I wished to thank you again for your support. I do know that Lady Catherine cares for her daughter but I believe Anne has changed since her accident."

Mr. Darcy was sorry for the man. Being berated by his aunt was a terrible way for the man to be treated when all he'd done was what he thought best for the young ladies under his care. "Dr. Green, I believe your presence has wrought a great change in my cousin, and her mother must see it as well. Aunt Catherine has kept Anne locked away for too many years. And her strong suspicions regarding the Bennet sisters are not unwarranted, though I would never admit such to her."

Dr. Green was surprised by Mr. Darcy's candor. He had not meant to discuss the matter of the Bennet sisters, for it was not proper. But even he had become suspicious after Lady Catherine's outburst. He'd not thought anything of the pairings before the scene in the parlor.

There was an equal number of gentlemen present to entertain the ladies, but with Miss Anne as his distraction there was little wonder why he hadn't thought more of it. Lady Catherine's conjecture regarding the sisters and her nephews coupled with Mr. Darcy's admission left little doubt. "Your aunt did mention to me that you are to marry your lovely cousin. I wished to speak with you on the matter but it is plain now that you are of the same mind as Miss Anne when it comes to her mother's wishes."

Mr. Darcy was not surprised his aunt had informed the man privately of her scheme. She'd taken every opportunity to speak of it since he'd arrived in Kent. "I do love my cousin, she is as a sister to me, but we shall never be wed. If my aunt has her way, poor Anne will live her life as a spinster. I have hopes that Georgie and I shall bring her to London once my aunt accepts that her plans will never be."

Dr. Green could not keep the truth from the gentleman before him. "Mr. Darcy, I fear I must speak truthfully. After your aunt impressed upon me the certainty of your betrothal to Miss Anne, I knew my hand would be forced. You see, I have fallen in love with your cousin. I rushed to her rooms earlier after speaking with your aunt and proposed to her."

Mr. Darcy could scarce believe his ears. He chuckled quietly at first but soon he was laughing out loud and the Fitzwilliam brothers turned as one to find the source of his amusement. Dr. Green was terrified the man might share his secret but Mr. Darcy waved his cousins back to their game and slowly regained his composure.

The poor doctor was mystified by his reaction. "Mr. Darcy, I should not have shared such foolish news with you. I ought to have known it was too soon to speak of my love for her, but what can be done now?"

The man was miserable and Mr. Darcy rushed to reassure him. "Chin up, old man. I am not laughing because of your actions. No, that is not the cause for merriment on my part. I simply imagined Aunt Catherine's face when she finds her daughter has been wooed by a physician. I see now why Anne said she would follow you to London. 'Tis not for your professional care of her person but for your care of her heart."

Dr. Green's countenance was one of comic relief and Mr. Darcy fought not to laugh at the poor man again. "I shall do all that I might to smooth the way for your marriage to my cousin. As for the timing, love is not bound by the ticking of a clock or the turning of seasons. When you first behold the face of your beloved the question is not whether you have loved her long enough, for your heart knows you have loved her always. The question is whether you shall have enough years to make her know the depths of that love."

Harry Green thought Mr. Darcy sounded like a man in love himself but decided not to pursue the matter. It was all the better for his courtship with

Miss Anne if Lady Catherine was distracted by the Bennet sisters.

"I would say that you must not address this issue with Aunt Catherine, not at the present time, as she will certainly have you removed from Rosings. Only take great care in your courtship of my cousin. Though my aunt is distracted by the Bennet sisters, it would not be wise to flaunt your love for Anne."

The doctor nodded his agreement and rose from his seat as Mr. Darcy stood. Before they might join the Fitzwilliam brothers at chess, he shook Mr. Darcy's hand. "Thank you, sir, for the advice and for not thinking me a fool to pursue your cousin."

༄

In Lady Catherine's study, Margaret Fitzwilliam sat patiently as she listened to the woman's complaints. Coming to speak with her about the concerns she held for Richard had been a decision she now nearly regretted.

"Once that doctor has gone, the Bennet sisters shall return to the parsonage and I will not abide their presence in my home again. Mark my words, Margaret, those two are fortune hunters! Your concern for Richard only strengthens my suspicions."

Since she was in for a penny, Lady Matlock decided to be in for a pound. "But what might we do in the meantime, Catherine? The doctor will not be moved in his decision and with Darcy supporting him, things will go on as they have."

Lady Catherine was pleased to have an ally at last. "Perhaps we might keep Richard and Darcy occupied? I shall say that I am not well enough to ride about the grounds with my steward and send them out. James has already become accustomed to it and he will surely encourage them to ride along."

Lady Matlock was not entirely certain the plan might work but if they were able to have the men away for hours each day, there would be less opportunity for the Bennet sisters to sit with the gentlemen. "I believe it might all be for naught, but we must try something. I shall have a word with Richard and see that he is not harboring feelings for Miss Bennet. As for Darcy, he does as he pleases and nothing I might say would make a difference."

Satisfied with their plan, Lady Catherine rose from her seat. "Leave Darcy to me, I am certain he will reconsider his options once I remind him that he stands to lose Rosings if he continues to defy me."

Lady Matlock would not speak again on the matter and took her leave of the study. Instead of interrupting the men in the library, she returned to the parlor with the ladies.

Miss Elizabeth and Miss Bennet were happily engaged in giving a play for her nieces and she paused in the doorway to watch. The Bennet sisters were quite witty. She found it such a pity their connections were not the kind her family would approve.

From her short time in the company of the Bennet sisters, she had come to admire them both though it meant little in the scheme of things. James would wed Sophia Cort and there was no question of that alliance. But Richard must marry almost as well as his brother.

Pushing away her thoughts, Lady Matlock made her way into the parlor and sat with her nieces. They all gave a rousing round of applause to the Bennet sisters as the ladies finished their humorous recital. "I say, I have never seen such a lively display by two young ladies."

Anne's countenance was one of great pride in her friends. "Aunt Margaret, Miss Elizabeth and Miss Bennet are well read and have a fondness for the bard. I believe before they depart Kent I shall have to stand with them and recite a part."

Miss Darcy was eager to make herself a part of the small company. "I would as well! I have never had such agreeable company as the Bennet sisters."

Turning to Elizabeth and Jane, Miss Darcy made a heartfelt plea that perturbed her aunt as the poor girl practically gave an open invitation to the sisters that extended far beyond tea. "When we have returned to Town, you must come to Darcy House as often as you wish for it is so lonely there."

Lady Matlock hid her agitation with her niece and patted the young lady's hand. "Now, Georgie, we do not know their plans in London. They have their own schedules to keep."

Elizabeth looked to Jane and chose her words carefully. "Miss Darcy, Jane and I would love to visit you in Town. You may always visit us at Cheapside if you wish. Before we depart, I will give you the address of our uncle's townhouse."

Pleased with her new friends, Miss Darcy turned to Lady Matlock. "Won't it be wonderful? I shall have company in London and perhaps Brother will ask them to Pemberley as well?"

Lady Matlock could not express her reservations in a way that would not upset her niece and so she merely agreed. "It cannot hurt for you to have companions in Town and the Bennets are such good friends already."

Elizabeth forced a smile as she caught the tone of Lady Matlock's words. The woman wished to please her niece but Elizabeth doubted she wished for the Darcys to be better acquainted with her or her sister.

CHAPTER 24

At dinner that evening, with a tone that showed she would not be questioned, Lady Catherine announced her plan for the Fitzwilliam brothers and Mr. Darcy. "I fear I am not well and must leave the management of the fields in your capable hands. How wonderful to have all my nephews present to assist in my time of need."

Dr. Green spoke up, his expression one of genuine concern. "I must insist upon offering my services, Lady Catherine. I could perform an examination after dinner if you like."

Lady Catherine gave a withering glance to the man. "That will not be necessary Dr. Green. I am well aware of my infirmity as my own physician has told me of it and how I must rest until the trouble has passed. I shall send my lady's maid to Hunsford on the morrow to the apothecary. He will know what to do."

Dr. Green thought it odd that the lady would not avail herself of his services but would not press the issue in front of her guests at dinner. He made note to see that she was not terribly ill in the morning when he rose.

Darcy was not moved by his aunt's request nor her vague excuse of ill health. He'd been a guest at Rosings far too many times in the past to believe his aunt had developed some mysterious ailment. "I shall be happy to accompany your steward on another day but I promised the ladies we might have a picnic on the morrow if the weather is fine."

Lady Catherine glanced at Lady Matlock before addressing Darcy's reluctance to do her bidding. "Fitzwilliam, I am not accustomed to being denied and of all my nephews, you are the most experienced with managing an estate of this size."

"Your steward ought to know more than I about the running of Rosings. I have full confidence that James and Richard shall be equal to the task with his assistance," Mr. Darcy turned his attention to his soup signaling he was finished with the topic of conversation.

Seeing her nephew would not be argued out of

his position, she turned her attention to Dr. Green. "Do you think it wise that Miss Anne should be wandering about in the fields on a picnic?"

Dr. Green looked to his beloved. "It appears that Miss Anne is well this evening. Barring any illness in the night, I cannot say why she must remain indoors. I commend Mr. Darcy for arranging such a delightful pastime."

Lady Catherine's jaw clenched and Lady Matlock braced herself for another tirade. She had warned the woman that Darcy would not be her pawn.

The mistress of Rosings glanced about the table taking the measure of the happy young people carrying on conversation and enjoying their meal. Never in her life had Darcy defied her, except for the matter of his marriage to Anne.

As her gaze took in the pairings in her dining room, Lady Catherine noted that although Miss Elizabeth was seated next to the doctor, her gaze often went to Darcy who was seated next to her sister. Likewise, her nephew Richard seemed preoccupied in his conversation but his gaze wandered far too frequently to Miss Bennet.

Lady Catherine was so distracted by the flirting of those two couples at her table that she did not catch the glances that flew between her daughter and Dr. Green.

Lady Matlock did not miss the sparkle in her niece's eye whenever she looked at Dr. Green, but she did not think it more serious than the infatuation of a young lady kept locked away for too long.

Focusing instead on her second son, Lady Matlock knew it would not do for him to believe that he might marry anyone he pleased without a thought for her dowry or connections.

The Earl of Matlock had apparently not impressed upon his second son the importance of choosing a wife from among the families of the Ton. Part of that difficulty stemmed from the fact that he was a soldier and had never yet seemed quite ready to marry.

As the young people stood to quit the dining room, Anne accepted Dr. Green's arm and waited as first Lady Catherine, escorted by James, and then Lady Matlock, escorted by Richard, led the party to the parlor.

Mr. Darcy gave an arm to his sister and offered the other to Miss Elizabeth but she shook her head and linked arms with Jane instead. Soon the ladies were left alone in the parlor while the gentlemen retired to the library for port.

Lady Catherine, still perturbed by Darcy's refusal to go out into the fields on the morrow, glared at the Bennet sisters. There was an awkward silence in the room and Miss Darcy rose quickly to seek her seat at the piano forte in the hope of distracting her aunt. Turning to Lady Catherine, she attempted to appear cheerful. "I would play for you the new music Brother gave me for my birthday if you it pleases you Aunt Catherine."

Turning to glance at her niece, Lady Catherine gave a cold smile that only hastened the girl's steps. "There are few people in England who have more true enjoyment of music than myself. If I had ever learnt, I should have been a great proficient. And so would Anne, if her health would have allowed her to apply. I am confident that she would have performed delightfully."

Elizabeth was pleased when at last Miss Darcy began to play. As the melody lifted, Lady Catherine turned to her. "I often tell young ladies that no excellence in music is to be acquired, Miss Elizabeth, without constant practice. Do you play?"

Elizabeth gave a pained smile. She had hoped in vain that the efforts of Miss Darcy might deliver her from Lady Catherine's notice. "I am not an expert, your ladyship. I fear it is my own fault as I have not taken the trouble to practice as I ought."

This admission seemed to give the lady some measure of satisfaction. "You shall never play really well unless you practice, young lady. To excel at music, you cannot play too often and if you have not studied under a master, well, that should be your first consideration."

Jane rose from her seat before the woman might ask about her musical proficiency and went to stand beside Miss Darcy as she played.

Though Lady Catherine continued her advice to Elizabeth, Jane began to sing along with the melody and soon the ladies had all turned to behold the eldest Bennet sister in her performance.

Jane's face grew hot but she continued along and Elizabeth was quite proud. Jane's singing voice was that of an angel and she was not the least surprised when the men drifted into the parlor to listen.

When the music ended, Richard Fitzwilliam called for her to perform another song and Miss Darcy gave her encouragement. "Yes, please Miss Jane! I would love to accompany you once more."

Jane could not refuse them and so she sang again and kept her eyes on the man of her dreams for most of the song. For his part, Richard Fitzwilliam was the picture of a man drawn to a woman as inevitably as a sailor is drawn to a siren.

Lady Matlock knew in that moment she had lost her son to Jane Bennet and nothing she might say would cause him to reconsider. She began to think of how she might embellish the girl's connections when speaking to her husband of their son's preference. She thought she recalled that Miss Bennet had said her uncle in Hertfordshire was a lawyer and her aunt in London came from gentry near Lambton.

As she thought it, Lady Matlock knew her husband would never accept such rubbish as to consider Miss Jane Bennet on par with the cream of the Ton. Still, Richard was her son and since James had done as expected she and the earl might be wise to simply accept the wishes of their headstrong son.

CHAPTER 25

O<small>N THE NEXT AFTERNOON</small>, Elizabeth released her ball upon the bowling green aiming perfectly for the white jack. Miss Darcy gave her a swift embrace as her ball stopped within inches of the white ball that was the target of the game. "Miss Elizabeth, you did not say you were practiced at bowls!"

Laughing merrily, Elizabeth glanced to Mr. Darcy as he strode toward them. The picnic and lawn games had been a most welcome treat and throughout the afternoon, the young guests of Rosings had made the most of the sunny day that seemed impossibly warm for the season.

Shielding her eyes, Elizabeth looked across the verdant bowling green to her sister. Colonel Fitzwilliam had returned from the fields with his brother in time to partake in the fun and was now showing Jane how to aim for the jack.

Lady Catherine and Lady Matlock remained indoors and Elizabeth was certain they were most unhappy with the frivolity that now ensued on the grounds of Rosings.

Miss Darcy greeted her brother before returning to the shade of the large tent the servants had erected earlier in the day. Elizabeth longed to follow as the heat of the day intensified with the sun at its zenith.

Mr. Darcy turned to her after watching his sister take James Fitzwilliam's arm. "Miss Elizabeth, would you care to join me under the tent? A young lady must not endure such a strong sun this time of the afternoon without a bonnet."

As she took his offered arm in reply, Mr. Darcy admired the blush of exertion that colored her cheeks. Wisps of her hair had fallen from their pins in an attractive manner about her neck. She smelled alluringly of lavender and light exertion. Her eyes danced merrily as he realized he had stared a moment too long.

"Mr. Darcy, is there something wrong sir?"

He smiled then, a broad and beautiful smile that came from the fullness of his heart. "Everything is as it should be Miss Elizabeth. I find great comfort in your company."

Elizabeth knew the sentiment well. The days at Rosings in his company among their mingled relations had passed much too quickly but now the secret she held from him diminished that comfort while she was in his presence.

Walking alongside Mr. Darcy with measured steps, Elizabeth longed to make her heart known to him before they reached the aim of their stroll. "Mr. Darcy, I find I quite agree with your sentiment. But there is more, much more, and I fear I must not say it yet."

Mr. Darcy turned, his expression one of great concern. "Miss Elizabeth, has something of that night returned to you? Perhaps if we speak with Dr. Green..."

Elizabeth hated that she had worried him. She lifted her hand to caress the line of his jaw before she thought better of her actions and drew it away. Mr. Darcy caught her hand and held it for a painfully sweet moment against his cheek. He moved to shield her from the view of the tent and Elizabeth's heart raced in her chest.

She wished to look away from his gaze but it bound her to him. "Mr. Darcy...it does not matter, not truly. With or without my memory, I am Elizabeth Bennet and I have grown quite fond of you."

Her voice was barely above a whisper and Mr. Darcy fought the urge to press his lips to hers and seal their fate. "When did you know your feelings for me, my dearest Elizabeth?"

His lady moved closer to him, testing his resolve and he dipped his head to be nearer. Her scent, the mingling of lavender with the warmth of the sun combined in a way he would always associate with her and this moment. Her lips parted and he waited for each word as a man awaiting the first sip of cool water in the desert.

Elizabeth's eyes searched his face, marking each line and plane. "I cannot fix on the hour, or the spot, or the look, or the words, which laid the foundation. It is too long ago. I was in the middle before I knew that I *had* begun."

Colonel Fitzwilliam's laughter startled the love-struck couple from their romantic moment and Elizabeth stepped away from Mr. Darcy tucking the hand that had rested against his cheek into a pocket of her skirt. Her palm tingled at the separation and Elizabeth breathed deeply to combat the dizziness that overtook her.

Mr. Darcy saw her sway and moved quickly. As

Richard and Jane approached, he swept her into his arms. Elizabeth's body went limp and Mr. Darcy strode quickly across the brilliant green of the lawn to deliver her into the doctor's care. "Come Harry, something has happened to Miss Elizabeth!"

Dr. Green left Anne's side and rushed to see to his patient. Elizabeth's head fell against Mr. Darcy's chest and the man became quite agitated. "Something must be done, she is not well!"

Jane moved to one of the tables arranged beneath the tent and pulled a fine linen tablecloth free of its home. Her voice was calm as she spread the rich white fabric upon the ground. "Place her here Mr. Darcy, we must not waste a moment."

As Mr. Darcy and Dr. Green saw to her sister, Jane turned to a maid and sent her for cool water and a cloth. Colonel Fitzwilliam busied himself with the pulling of a chair closer to the place where Elizabeth lay. "Let us get her feet up, doctor. I've seen my men in the field get the legs of those injured above the head, something to do with aiding the flow of blood."

Jane moved to her sister's feet and performed the service so as to preserve Elizabeth's dignity. Dr. Green lowered his ear to listen for the sighs of breath that puffed quickly from his patient. He watched her chest rise and fall and worried perhaps the heat had caused her distress.

Mr. Darcy fell to his knees on the other side of his love and looked helplessly at her still form. The scene was much too vivid and his mind could only envision her limp and injured in the back of that wagon.

Dr. Green urged the rest of their party to move away and Mr. Darcy took Elizabeth's hand as Jane kneeled beside him. "She will come around Mr. Darcy, do not fear."

Elizabeth Bennet could hear the murmurs around her but she was not able to speak with her head spinning as it was now. It was a trial to breathe and the voices of her loved ones under the tent grew fuzzy except for the voice of Mr. Darcy.

She watched as he stood before her, his face lit with adoration. They seemed to be in Charlotte's parlor and Elizabeth thought she must have fallen asleep. How terribly embarrassing!

Mr. Darcy's words penetrated her mortification. "I would have you as my wife, my Elizabeth, and count myself a happy man to endure the sneers of society at our unlikely pairing."

As she gasped for air in surprise, the entire scene played out before her and Elizabeth felt her heart squeeze painfully in her chest at the terrible manner in which she had refused the man. Mr. Darcy loved her and wanted to marry her! Certainly he had not known the words to say to a lady he wished to marry but she found she could forgive him that.

Before she could reach out to the dream Darcy and accept him at last, Charlotte came into view.

The parlor dissolved along with Mr. Darcy and they were standing outside the parsonage in the waning light of the evening. Charlotte spoke of Elizabeth's prejudice against Mr. Darcy because of the trouble with Mr. Bingley and Jane and Wickham's sad tale. Elizabeth wanted to run, to escape the torture of what she'd done to Mr. Darcy but her feet would not move.

The Charlotte in her dream moved closer and hugged her tightly. "Oh Lizzy, you have been wrong about Mr. Darcy and now you must speak with him if only to offer an apology. He is a good man, one you deserve though you may think you do not. Come, let us go in before Mr. Collins finds us here on the doorstep behaving as foolish girls. On the morrow, I will go with you to Rosings to right this wrong."

Elizabeth's eyes flew open then as she struggled to breath. Mr. Darcy and Dr. Green were on either side of her while Jane was kneeling by her head applying a wonderfully cool cloth to her brow.

Colonel Fitzwilliam steered Miss Anne and Miss Darcy away from the scene as Dr. Green checked her pupils before laying the back of his hand against her forehead. "Are you well, Miss Elizabeth? You gave us quite the scare."

She smiled to show the man she was quite alright. Never in her life had she come close to fainting. Elizabeth Bennet was a great walker and accustomed to rambling outdoors for hours on days much warmer than this one.

The swoon had been induced by the heat and the nearness of Mr. Darcy, though she would not admit the part Mr. Darcy played before the physician. "I am sorry, Dr. Green. It must have been the heat."

Jane helped her to sit and gave her the glass of cool water the maid had brought. Elizabeth busied herself with drinking to avoid Mr. Darcy's gaze. His pained expression haunted Elizabeth and she was sorry to have caused him such concern.

Dr. Green returned to Miss Anne's side to assure the ladies and Colonel Fitzwilliam that his patient was well. Jane moved away after helping Elizabeth to stand and regain her dignity.

Elizabeth breathed deeply to control the emotions that churned in her breast at having recalled that afternoon in the parlor and the subsequent intervention of her friend Charlotte.

How might she speak with Mr. Darcy about love when she'd refused him so horribly? Knowing she must, but wishing to preserve the romantic feelings now growing between them, Elizabeth decided she would simply wait though it was nearly impossible to look at the man and not confide in him.

Mr. Darcy retrieved the linen tablecloth from the ground and handed it to the maid. His eyes still held the worry she'd seen upon awaking on her back. "Miss Elizabeth, I would be happy to escort you back to the house and stay with you there."

His concern touched her heart. "No, I would stay here under the tent and dine with you. I promise I am not a wilting flower, Mr. Darcy," here her voice lowered to a conspiratorial whisper and he bent his head closer to hers, "twas your fault I became breathless to begin with."

Mr. Darcy forgot the worry that went before and was pleased with his effect upon the lady. In the future he would be certain she was sitting when the desire to make mad love to her overwhelmed his better judgment. He teased her mercilessly as he longed to kiss her lips. "I promise never to leave you breathless again, Miss Elizabeth."

Her brow furrowed at this terrible vow. "Mr. Darcy, do not make such a promise for you cannot keep it. It is not in your power to control. Your mere presence is enough to steal the air from my lungs."

Elizabeth gazed at him daring him to kiss her. When it seemed he might take her challenge, she took his hand and pulled him to the tables where their party sat ready to dine.

Mr. Darcy was transported by her words, his mind conjuring scenes of her at Pemberley in his bed, in the chair that matched his own in the library across from him as they read together, of her heavy with their first child.

He would propose to her again and pray that his past sins were forgotten never to haunt them again.

CHAPTER 26

AFTER THE PICNIC AND GAMES, when everyone was satisfied that Elizabeth had recovered, the young ladies performed their play for the gentlemen in the parlor and there was much merriment and laughter that drifted across the hallway to the study where Lady Matlock had been summoned by Lady Catherine.

The sound of the gaiety of young people wore on Lady Catherine's nerves. She rose to slam the door of her study in her agitation. "There is nothing to be done now but to remove the Bennet sisters from my home! I do not care what Dr. Green believes, they shall leave this very night."

Lady Matlock knew there was no reasoning with the woman and frankly, she did not wish to intervene. Her sons had made quick work of their ride about the fields with the steward and the picnic had lasted well into the afternoon. When the couples returned, she and Catherine had spent but half an hour in the parlor before Georgiana had suggested the play.

Lady Catherine had pretended at illness once more when presented with the high spirits of her young guests and quit the parlor. Now, the pair sat stewing in the dreary study and Margaret Fitzwilliam was weary of the incessant complaining by her sister-in-law. A full hour in the study that was more of a lair left her without the patience to continue her visit.

Standing and smoothing her skirts before quitting the dim interior of the study, Lady Matlock spoke her piece. "Do as you wish, Catherine. Darcy shall simply visit Miss Elizabeth at the cottage or in Town when everyone has left Kent. I believe I ought to return to London with Richard and James on the morrow. At least Richard shall be parted from Miss Bennet for a time that way."

Lady Catherine called her butler to her side and ordered him to ready a carriage to see the Bennet sisters to the parsonage. "They shall leave shortly but first I must gather my papers to speak with Darcy.

Leave me now and do not alert my guests of my plans. They shall know soon enough."

Lady Matlock made her way to the library to await her sons for she knew they would smoke their horrible cigars before dinner. Upon entering the room, the surprise at finding Richard and Darcy already there flitted across her face but she quickly hid it in favor of a more severe expression.

The two gentlemen rose from their chairs and waited until she took her seat. Without preamble, she spoke before they might sit again. "Darcy, I would speak with Richard alone."

Before Darcy might tamp out his cigar, Richard held up a hand. "Mother, whatever you might say I believe it must involve the Bennet sisters and I am certain you wish for Darcy to know it."

Mr. Darcy was not the least bit keen to know what his aunt thought of the ladies. "I would not stay and listen, Richard. There is nothing that would alter my feelings for either sister."

Lady Matlock snapped at them to sit and both men obeyed without further question. They might be grown men of the world, but Margaret Fitzwilliam was at the end of her patience. "I believe in Darcy's case there is nothing I might say though Catherine surely may before the night is over." She gave her nephew a pointed gaze before continuing, "Let that be a warning to you, son."

Mr. Darcy looked to his cousin and decided to hold his opinion and allow his aunt to speak on the matter. There was no need to irritate her further.

"Richard, we shall leave on the morrow after breaking our fast. Catherine has said the Bennet sisters may not stay a moment longer but I informed her that removing them to the parsonage will not be a deterrent where you and Darcy are concerned."

Seeing there was no reason to avoid his mother's knowledge of his feelings for Miss Bennet, Richard drew a long puff on his cigar to gather his thoughts before speaking. "Mother, I do intend to seek Miss Bennet's hand at some time in the future. I shall report to my superior officers in London and submit my resignation. But I will not leave this house without making known my intentions where she is concerned."

Lady Matlock smiled coldly at her second son. She had never expected him to relinquish his life as a soldier so soon but love made many a man give up dreams that paled in comparison to a young lady's beauty. "I would caution you, son. Your father shall not be happy. I have thought of how I might portray your intended's connections and small dowry to her advantage but honestly, your father will not be fooled. I am certain he will be in no mood to settle the same sum to your account as he would have had you chosen more wisely."

Mr. Darcy stood and began to pace the library as Richard remained silent. "Aunt Margaret, though I ought to mind my tongue in this matter, I am compelled to note the estate that shall fall to Richard is quite capable of providing a living well beyond that of a soldier. He would be able to easily provide for a wife and several children."

Richard spoke up after Darcy finished. "I had never thought to be denied my rightful place in the family behind James and as my cousin has said, the estate promised to me shall provide a handsome living."

Lady Matlock eyed the two men. They had spoken of this matter before — Richard's plans for himself and Miss Bennet. She wondered how it was that her most judicious and practically minded son had fallen so quickly in love. "Richard, I cannot promise that your father's wrath will not be so great that he is driven to withhold the estate from you as well."

Colonel Fitzwilliam stood and looked to Darcy before beginning his own circuit from his chair to the fireplace. "Mother, if Father should hold such anger for me there is little I might do to change his mind. I will not give up Miss Bennet. I could offer her a life as a soldier's wife and she has some small dowry of her own. It will not be as comfortable an existence as she has previously led but I shall leave the decision to her."

Margaret Fitzwilliam had known her second son would not be moved by the truth she laid before him. Persuading his father not to disown him would require a bit of finesse on her part since she had put it in the earl's mind to control Richard through the promise of money should he marry well. With deep regret, Lady Matlock stood and waited until her son came to her.

"I am not certain that I will succeed, Richard, but I shall do all that I might to aid in your folly. Your father will be quite angry and you must prepare for that, but in time I believe I might persuade him to forgive you. Of all things, the worst for him would be the gossip in Town were he to leave you and your wife penniless."

Colonel Fitzwilliam startled his mother by pulling her into a bear hug and lifting her off her feet. "Let us worry about Father after Miss Bennet has accepted my proposal."

Lady Matlock demanded he set her down again, though her expression was one of delight at her son's display of affection. "If she shuns you, I shall never forgive her. I would not speak of challenging your father nor argue with you for naught."

Richard's booming laughter followed his mother as she quit the library. Darcy resumed his seat and thought how fortunate he was not to have to worry about his selection of Miss Elizabeth for his wife. The only person against him was his Aunt Catherine and her opinion held as much weight as a stranger as far as he was concerned.

In the hallway outside the library, Lady Matlock saw the Bennet sisters standing by the parlor door. "Ladies, has the play ended? I am sorry to have missed it. I've rarely heard such merriment within the walls of Rosings."

Elizabeth and Jane wondered at the woman's change of attitude. Jane took the woman's hand and turned towards the room where Miss Anne and Miss Darcy still sat chattering away at their accomplishment. "Perhaps your nieces would recite their parts for you again, Lady Matlock, if you come with me."

The lady accepted Jane's invitation and the pair left Elizabeth in the hallway. She thought of joining them but she wanted desperately to speak with Mr.

Darcy. The time had come for her to confess to him all that she'd remembered under the tent and find whether he might still wish to marry her.

Elizabeth moved toward the library and the voices of Mr. Darcy and Colonel Fitzwilliam drifted into the hallway. She stood before the door and gathered her courage. Before she might knock upon the heavy, polished wood, Richard's voice halted her steps and she clapped a hand over her mouth to keep from crying out with joy.

"Darcy, I intend to ask Miss Bennet for her hand this night. Aunt Catherine will not wait to send them to the parsonage and Mother is set on leaving come morning."

Mr. Darcy grunted and lowered his voice. "Richard, you must take care. Miss Bennet is not one to share her deepest feelings as most ladies might when they are in love. You must be certain she is the woman you wish to marry before you anger your father."

Elizabeth could not believe her ears. Mr. Darcy was warning his cousin against a match with Jane! The words hung in the air for a moment too long without a reply from Richard and Elizabeth forced her feet to carry her into the library. "Mr. Darcy, I came to speak with you about your visit the day of the accident and I find you warning your cousin against Jane! Was it not enough that you warned Mr. Bingley away from her? How could I love you when you hurt my sister again and again?"

Richard and Darcy moved as one to reach her but Elizabeth turned and ran from the library, tears pouring down her cheeks. She would leave here tonight with Jane and never return!

In her anger, Elizabeth hurried to the parlor door. "Jane, come quick! We must go now to the parsonage. I will not stay here another moment."

Lady Catherine appeared at the commotion as Richard and Mr. Darcy surrounded Elizabeth and a footman came down the stairs with Jane's trunk.

Before Mr. Darcy might plead his case, Lady Catherine signaled the footman toward the front door. "A carriage awaits to take them to the parsonage. I am pleased to see them go but I am surprised that Miss Elizabeth would leave of her own accord."

Mr. Darcy lashed out at his aunt, his anger boiling over. "You have no heart, Aunt Catherine! The Bennet sisters have done nothing to draw your ire. It is me you wish to punish! Instead you plot to have them removed in the night like a cowardly, small villain."

Lady Matlock gasped at this and tried to shield

Miss Anne and Miss Darcy who were now quite upset by the spectacle before them.

Elizabeth was sobbing in Jane's arms as Darcy turned away from his aunt to speak with her. "My dearest Elizabeth, you do not understand what you overheard. I would never come between my cousin and your sister. You must believe me."

Lady Catherine moved to stand between Darcy and the Bennet sisters. "Let them go, Fitzwilliam. They are no longer welcome here!"

Jane looked to Richard, her lovely blue eyes full of doubt and questions she could not ask. She turned and led her inconsolable sister into the night toward the waiting carriage. Mr. Darcy's voice thundered behind them and Jane quickened her steps. No matter the misunderstanding, she would not remain at Rosings with her sister.

"Elizabeth! Elizabeth! You cannot go now before you know the truth! Please hear me out!"

Richard struggled to keep Darcy from dashing after the sisters. They were only going to the parsonage after all and the misunderstanding was an easy one to sort. "Come away, Darcy. Miss Elizabeth is not in any shape to argue with you this night. We shall see them on the morrow together."

Lady Catherine slammed the front door of

Rosings and bore down on her nephews. "Richard, you have led Darcy astray into the hands of that country chit that would destroy our family! How has your mother allowed such disobedience and foolishness?"

Richard's voice thundered through the entryway drowning out the worried whispers of his female cousins. "Aunt Catherine, you have no right..."

Before her son might give his aunt the dressing down she deserved, Lady Matlock stepped between them. "Catherine, Richard is a grown man and has made his own decision regarding who he will marry. It is high time you understood you cannot bend my sons, nor your daughter, to your will."

CHAPTER 27

Jane comforted Elizabeth as best she could on the way to the parsonage. Mr. Collins would be furious at their situation, being thrown out of Rosings by his patroness in the night was surely a terrible offense and one that might cost him his living.

Instead of worrying about the coming trials, Jane pulled Elizabeth closer and whispered desperately in the darkness of the carriage. "Shhh...Lizzy, please. We have to think. What was it that Mr. Darcy said?"

Elizabeth took the handkerchief that Jane thrust into her hands and buried her face in the gently scented linen. Her mind was a terribly confused muddle.

Allowing the embrace of her sister to comfort her, Elizabeth sighed and tried to settle her thoughts.

"Jane, he did it again. He warned the Colonel away from you just as he did with Mr. Bingley."

Jane could not believe her sister's words. "You must be mistaken Lizzy. Mr. Darcy has been nothing but kind and defended us against Lady Catherine's every barb. Miss Darcy and Miss Anne told me he would not listen to a word against us. And Richard Fitzwilliam is not the kind of man to be easily swayed even if Mr. Darcy advised him I was a poor match. But if they were speaking of me then that means he was thinking of proposing!"

Jane's voice rose above a whisper and Elizabeth was sorry to have given her the news of Richard's intentions in such a terrible manner. "Lizzy! Do you believe he might ask for my hand in marriage? It is simply too much to hope for. I do love him so."

Elizabeth was miserable. She had betrayed the confidence of Colonel Fitzwilliam in her weakness. Tears threatened once more but she bit her bottom lip to regain her composure. "Jane, I am a terrible sister to have revealed as much to you but I could not allow Mr. Darcy to ruin your happiness yet again. It was unbearable to hear him tell his cousin to be certain of his feelings before he angered his father by asking for your hand."

Jane's joyful expression fell and was replaced by

knitted brows of confusion. "Lizzy, Mr. Darcy's advice was sound. Of course Colonel Fitzwilliam should be certain before asking for my hand. It is only sensible to think such a thing since he is the second son. I cannot think his family will approve of my small dowry."

The carriage arrived and the footman helped the ladies down before he moved quickly to fetch Jane's trunk. Mr. Collins appeared at the door, for he had heard the carriage arrive. Charlotte came behind him, her hand flying to her mouth as she saw that it was Jane and Elizabeth in the lane with a footman holding a trunk.

Mr. Collins hurried to the gate. "What is the meaning of this Cousin Jane?"

His voice was strident and Charlotte lingered by the door instead of following her husband. She knew well enough when his voice reached such an octave it was best to remain quiet and unnoticed.

Elizabeth motioned the footman towards the cottage and spoke to Mr. Collins. "Lady Catherine wished for us to leave Rosings without delay. Of course, we obeyed her wishes."

Mr. Collins glanced from Elizabeth to Jane, his mouth gaping as a fish that has been caught and reeled from the stream. At last, he turned and looked to Charlotte. "I must go and see her ladyship and find why my cousins have been turned out so late in the evening. No doubt they have brought shame upon our family!"

The footman returned and briskly regained his post as Mr. Collins called to the driver. "Wait, wait for me. I would go to see her ladyship this instant!"

The driver halted his pull on the reins and waited as Mr. Collins climbed hastily inside the carriage his cousins had only just vacated. Before the door was shut behind the man, the driver flicked the reins and sent the horses into a turn where the road widened across from the cottage.

Elizabeth and Jane watched as their cousin was carried away to Rosings and knew their night would extend well into the early hours of the morning once he returned from an ill-advised visit with Lady Catherine.

Charlotte stirred by the door and rushed to the gate to welcome her friends. "Lizzy, Jane, do come inside. We must visit before Mr. Collins returns. I fear he shall be in a most terrible mood by then."

The Bennet sisters made haste to enter the cottage behind their dearest friend from Hertford-shire. Elizabeth began to worry that perhaps her cousin might lose his living at Hunsford.

Fighting the anger that rose in her breast at Lady Catherine, Elizabeth entered the parlor behind Jane and Charlotte. Her friend closed the door softly and beckoned for them to sit with her near the window on the far side of the room.

Charlotte sat and kept her hands tightly clasped in her lap. "Though I am happy to see you both, I must know what has happened before Mr. Collins returns. I fear it is not good news, not so late in the evening."

Jane looked to Elizabeth, for she did not wish to begin the tale. Only Elizabeth truly knew the particulars given her outburst with Mr. Darcy in the library.

Elizabeth held her head high, the tears gone and her mind clear. "There is much to tell, Charlotte. I will only say that I overheard Mr. Darcy speaking to Colonel Fitzwilliam in the library about his feelings for Jane. It was how he must have spoken to Mr. Bingley and I could not bear it, not when I had come to believe with all my heart that we might find happiness together."

Charlotte sat quietly for a moment as she observed her friend. The Elizabeth before her now was the same Elizabeth from the day of Mr. Darcy's proposal. Keeping her voice calm, Charlotte moved to sit closer to Elizabeth. "Lizzy, has your memory returned?"

Elizabeth had not wished to speak of it, but it was far too late now to hide. "Pieces of that day haunt me, but they have no bearing on the matter at hand."

Jane watched her sister with great interest but kept her silence as Charlotte continued to question Elizabeth. Clearly Elizabeth did not wish to speak of Mr. Darcy's proposal.

"Lizzy, your memory has much to do with the matter at hand. Mr. Darcy came to pay a call that day. Do you remember?"

Elizabeth closed her eyes and turned her head away. "Miss Anne asked a question before the accident. She asked whether I would leave him alone to think I did not care for him. I wanted to go to him that night but I knew Lady Catherine would be furious at me over her daughter."

Jane gasped and rose to go to her sister. "You knew you loved him that night?"

Charlotte took her friend's hand and removed the handkerchief. "Lizzy knew because I would not let her use Mr. Wickham nor Mr. Bingley as an excuse to deny Mr. Darcy."

A maid knocked upon the parlor door then and

soon the hallway outside the modest room was full with guests. Charlotte could see Colonel Fitzwilliam and Mr. Darcy behind the maid with Miss Anne pushing her way between them.

Lady Catherine and Mr. Collins were the last in the hallway behind Lady Matlock and Miss Darcy who were escorted by James Fitzwilliam and Dr. Green.

Turning to the Bennet sisters behind her, Charlotte had little choice but to stand aside and allow the party from Rosings to enter her small parlor.

Elizabeth stood and moved toward the door as the guests poured into the small space hoping she might escape to the relative safety of her upstairs room but Mr. Collins blocked her way. His expression was one Elizabeth had not seen on the man's face at any time in the past. He seemed quite beaten and subdued and yet there was a hint of malice in his tone as he admonished her. "You must stay until this mess is sorted, Cousin Elizabeth."

Lady Catherine and Lady Matlock were guided to the sofa by Charlotte while James and Dr. Green remained standing. Richard had gone to Jane's side to take her hand. At this, Lady Catherine began to berate the young couple.

Mr. Darcy was dismayed that his sister had been

swept into the confusion and brought along to the cottage but she was huddled at a table behind the sofa with their cousin Anne. There was no need to send her from the room for she had already heard quite enough of the arguments that had continued at Rosings after the Bennet sister's departure.

Instead, he turned to Miss Elizabeth fixing her with his gaze. He wanted to go to her and take her in his arms but he knew he must explain himself to her and declare his love yet again.

That it would occur in the company of all their friends and family did not appeal to him greatly but he would not leave the cottage a second time without an assurance from his lady that they would one day be man and wife. "Miss Elizabeth, I must insist upon addressing your charge in the library at Rosings."

Lady Catherine turned her attention to Darcy and waved a sheaf of papers she'd brought from Rosings. "Fitzwilliam! I swear to you that Rosings shall pass to Anne and be lost if you pursue this foolish notion of marrying that terrible girl! I will not leave it to you as we had agreed."

Anne rose from her seat and went to stand beside Dr. Green. "Mother, Rosings shall not be lost and Fitzwilliam shall not marry me. Harry and I will be wed."

Lady Catherine jumped from her seat as the room filled with exclamations of surprise at the announcement of Miss Anne de Bourgh. Miss Darcy dashed to her cousin's side and embraced her excitedly. "Shall we plan a wedding at Pemberley or perhaps in the gardens of Rosings?"

"There will be no wedding here nor there, Georgiana!" Lady Catherine's patience was now at an end. She advanced across the room to where her daughter stood with Dr. Green.

"You shall not marry a physician young lady! If your cousin will not heed my wishes, then I shall seek a suitable young gentleman from among the families of the Ton. Return to the carriage and wait for me. I shall not be long in taking my leave of this horrid cottage."

Dr. Green placed an arm about his betrothed and spoke with authority to her mother. "Your ladyship, with all respect due your station, I beseech you to give your blessing on our marriage. I would not come between a mother and daughter but I will not abandon my dear Anne, for I do love her."

Lady Catherine launched herself at the couple, a high shrill screech preceding her. James Fitzwilliam caught his aunt by the shoulders and pulled her away from the couple. "Aunt Catherine, you must not behave so in the home of your parson!"

Mr. Darcy went to his sister and escorted her from the parlor. He asked the maid to sit with her in the study until the terrible business in the parlor was settled.

"But Brother, I would not leave Anne alone with Aunt Catherine in such a temper!"

Mr. Darcy smoothed the loose curls from his sister's face and shook his head. "Anne is not alone, dear. We shall not allow Aunt Catherine to harm her more than she already has this night. Please, go with the maid. I promise we shall not be much longer."

Waiting until his sister disappeared into the small study, Mr. Darcy turned back to the parlor and squared his shoulders. He must remove his Aunt Catherine from the parsonage and send her back to Rosings.

He returned to the parlor and closed the door behind him. Turning his attention to Lady Catherine, he spoke out of concern for her health. "You must return to Rosings, for I fear you are not well enough to remain here arguing against that which you cannot change. There is much to be settled that you will certainly find offensive."

Charlotte Collins went to her husband's

patroness and motioned for Mr. Collins to follow. "Come, your ladyship. If you will not return to Rosings, you may sit in my dining room and I will listen to all that you have to say."

Mr. Collins came to stand beside his wife. "Your ladyship, I am most terribly sorrowful for all that has transpired. Had I known my cousins were the cause of such trouble I would have sent them home on the next post chaise."

Lady Catherine pushed past the parson and his wife, leaving a threat behind as she made her way to the parlor door. "I would not stay a moment longer under this roof! After such utter betrayal you may find yourselves in the hedgerows before dawn breaks."

Elizabeth watched as Charlotte and Mr. Collins hurried from the room following in Lady Catherine's wake. She had not thought Mr. Darcy might come to her at the parsonage with his entire family. The memory of Mr. Darcy's proposal returned as the man moved towards her.

In great distress, Elizabeth made her way to the door of the parlor though Mr. Darcy called her name softly. "My dearest Elizabeth, you must hear me out."

Instead, she slipped away through the door. Lady

Catherine was berating her cousin near the front door and Elizabeth turned away to rush to the kitchen so she might escape into the small garden behind the parsonage.

In her haste, she did not know that Mr. Darcy had followed her, his long stride easily keeping pace with her hurried footsteps. Once in the garden, she rushed to the low stone wall that bounded the property and began to scramble over the top.

Mr. Darcy caught her in his arms and Elizabeth gave a surprised yelp. "Mr. Darcy! Let me go!"

The blasted man ignored her command and turned to sit upon the wall still holding her easily with one arm. "I shall let you go if you promise to hear me out, my Elizabeth. When I have said all there is to say, you may stay and be my wife or jump this wall and disappear into the woods."

Elizabeth knew she should not agree to hear him out, but the warmth of his body against hers and the mention of becoming his wife gave her pause. Her thoughts swirled in her head until everything was a tangle of memory, desire, and confusion. She ceased her struggle to break free and bowed her head. "I will listen Mr. Darcy, I promise. But you must be patient. I remember your proposal that day."

Mr. Darcy did not wish to release Elizabeth

Bennet for her presence in his arms made his heart soar in his chest until he fought to maintain his composure. Placing her on her feet again, he would not release her hand as she gazed into his eyes. "I was hoping you would not remember it so well. I would give all that I own if it would make you forget that proposal entirely."

"I never want to forget any part of my life, Mr. Darcy, not even your proposal. One reason I could not accept you then was because of Jane. And when I overheard you warning your cousin to be certain of my sister, I could not believe I had come to love a man so determined to ruin my sister's chance at happiness."

Mr. Darcy understood perfectly well how his words to Richard in the library had upset his lady. "I made that mistake once and I would not make it again where your sister is concerned. I only advised Richard that his father's disapproval would be a hindrance to their future happiness and so he must be certain of Miss Bennet's feelings to present a united front to his parents. The Matlocks are good people, but as I struggled with my pride so shall they."

Elizabeth released the breath she had been

holding as he spoke. "So you aren't opposed to my sister marrying your cousin?"

Mr. Darcy pushed away a loose curl from Elizabeth's forehead. Grateful that she allowed him the opportunity to mend the rift between them, he did his best to address her concern. "It would not matter to Richard what I thought. He is a man who lives life on his own terms but he and Miss Bennet have my full support. If his father is foolish enough to withhold land and wealth from Richard, I shall see that he is settled with an estate near Pemberley."

Elizabeth moved into the circle of his arms and laid her head against his chest. Mr. Darcy was changed and when she thought of the day he'd tried to help her remember his visit to the parsonage, a great pride in the man swelled in her chest. He had been willing to risk losing her if it meant her peace of mind was restored. "You wanted to tell me of your proposal on the terrace when I was struggling with my memory didn't you?"

Mr. Darcy's expression was one of pain and sorrow. "I did, and I ought to have told you and trusted that whatever you decided would be enough. But I was scared, Elizabeth. Can you imagine *the* Fitzwilliam Darcy in such a state?"

A pitiful chuckle followed his words and Elizabeth looked up at him. She lifted a hand to caress his strong jaw. There was a tension there she wished to erase. "I cannot imagine my Darcy in such turmoil, sir. My Darcy is so kind and strong, so different from the man he was that day and all the days before."

Mr. Darcy caught her hand and placed a kiss inside the palm. "I am a different man and have been since the moment you arrived injured at Rosings in the back of that wagon. My Elizabeth," his voice broke with emotion and he paused to regain his composure, "by you, I was properly humbled. I came to you that day without a doubt of my reception. You showed me how insufficient were all my pretensions to please a woman worthy of being pleased. Nothing matters so much to me now as spending my life with you. You must allow me to make a proper proposal."

Elizabeth laid her head against his chest again. The rhythm of his heartbeat matched her own and she closed her eyes. "My Darcy, you have made the best proposal just now. I assure you that I am the one who was humbled. I thought you a man unworthy of my love and found instead my own failings."

Mr. Darcy meant to speak, to disabuse her of the notion that she was anything but perfect for him and so very worthy of his love, but Elizabeth looked up and placed a finger on his lips. "There is nothing more to say except I love you and I will marry you."

Mr. Darcy tipped her chin up to gaze into her fine eyes. "You must allow me to tell you how ardently I admire and love you."

Elizabeth smiled at him with a mischievous light in her eyes. "Show me Mr. Darcy, for words cannot explain love the way lips in supplication might. Kiss me and end all doubt. Make me know that I am yours."

Mr. Darcy needed no further enticement from his lady. Gently taking her face in both hands, he began with her forehead. His breath against her skin lit a fire in Elizabeth's body that soon consumed her as his lips moved to kiss the closed lids of her eyes in turn.

When he arrived at her lips, she sighed against the soft insistence of his kiss. Her knees grew weak and Mr. Darcy swept her into his arms as his demand for her kiss grew more insistent.

Elizabeth Bennet remained in the garden with Mr. Darcy until Colonel Fitzwilliam and Jane came looking for them with their own good news of another engagement.

EPILOGUE

THE GROUNDS of Pemberley were dotted with the tops of snow-white tents placed around the lake as Elizabeth Bennet Darcy climbed into the Darcy carriage, the one she'd avoided in Hunsford so many months ago, with the assistance of her husband Fitzwilliam Darcy.

Behind them, Dr. Harry Green helped his wife Anne into the carriage that would see them to London before they began their month long wedding trip.

Elizabeth looked ahead to the carriage from the Matlocks that would carry her sister, Jane Bennet Fitzwilliam, on her wedding trip with Colonel Fitzwilliam. They would spend a night in their country estate near Pemberley before leaving on the morrow for Scotland.

"Mr. Darcy, where shall we spend our days before returning to Pemberley? I could not persuade even one maid to give me a hint though I did bribe them handsomely."

Mr. Darcy laughed at his bride. He had known she would attempt to discover his plans and had not told anyone, save his valet, of their destination. "I have arranged for us to travel to Ramsgate and make our way to Sanditon, Brighton, and Weymouth before returning home."

Elizabeth clapped her hands in glee. "I have never been to the seaside Mr. Darcy! What a capital idea!"

Mr. Darcy stretched his legs as the carriage moved forward and smiled at his lovely bride. She was dressed in a pale pink satin that perfectly complimented her glowing skin.

He had made arrangements in London when they returned from Kent to have Georgiana's favorite modiste come to Darcy House to outfit his soon-to-be wife. He knew he would be most pleased with the results if this dress was any indication of the contents of the trunks the footmen had loaded that morning before the triple wedding ceremony in Pemberley's ballroom.

"I wish to stroll by the sea and take you out on a

boat where I would make mad, passionate love to you while the captain ignores us completely." Mr. Darcy took her hand and kissed the finger that bore the ring his father had given his mother on their wedding day.

Elizabeth drew in her breath as his lips brushed against her fingers. "Mr. Darcy, you must not tempt me so when we have so far to travel this day."

Dropping her hand, Mr. Darcy gave his bride a wicked smile and moved closer to her, his arm out to draw the drapes on her side of the carriage. "Mrs. Darcy," he whispered as he kissed her lips lightly, "I believe you shall find that this carriage is equipped for the most private of meetings."

Elizabeth gave a nervous laugh as he moved away to his side of the carriage to pull the heavy drapes there. Surely he meant only to tease her with amorous kisses and sweet words.

"Mr. Darcy, won't the footmen talk?" Elizabeth opened the fan Jane had given her before the wedding ceremony. It was made of feathers, like the blue one from their uncle's warehouse, but there were seed pearls scattered strategically here and there and the feathers were a creamy white that were most alluringly displayed against the skin of her neck as she positioned the fan and batted her eyelashes at her husband.

"The footmen shall talk if we make it ten miles down the road without pulling the drapes my dear. You see, they are married men and know the intense desire a husband holds on his wedding day for his wife."

Elizabeth trembled as Mr. Darcy pulled her into his arms. His lips traced a path from her ear down the side of her neck and she gave a tiny squeak at the passionate display from her husband.

"Mr. Darcy," she whispered, the silk in her voice inciting even more wanton behavior from her husband.

"Yes, my love," he replied as his hands slid over the fabric of her dress molding her curves with the warmth of his touch.

"What will they say if your passion overcomes your good sense, sir? Will they not know what you are about in here with the drapes drawn?"

Mr. Darcy growled as he pulled his wife onto his lap. "Forget the footmen, woman. They are paid not to think anything I might do is their concern."

Elizabeth closed her eyes as Mr. Darcy's hands removed the delicate slippers from her feet. She had not thought what a man and wife might do inside a carriage as luxurious and well-sprung as this but her imagination was quickly being supplied with ardent examples as Mr. Darcy whispered words of love and worshipped her face and lips with sweet, urgent kisses.

At once, she wondered whether Colonel Fitzwilliam was behaving in the same manner and bit back the giggle that formed in her throat. The man had never been shy with his praise of her sister's form so Elizabeth could only think he was at least as playful as Mr. Darcy.

Sighing as her husband became poetic over the shape of her calves, Elizabeth leaned into his kisses and returned them in a manner that undid what little control Mr. Darcy still possessed.

The footmen at the back of the Darcy carriage shared a knowing glance when a muffled moan from their master, and a feminine giggle, drifted to them on the warm summer air. Their master had brought home a lovely lass with a charming smile and boundless energy. They knew soon the halls of Pemberley would once again hold the noise of many children.

ABOUT THE AUTHOR

April Floyd is a wanderer of the world and lover of great stories who now resides in the Last Frontier with her husband and youngest child. As a reader, she adores JAFF, dystopian fiction, historical fiction, and all types of nonfiction but holds a fondness for the topic of British grand estates and homes.

www.authoraprilfloyd.com
authoraprilfloyd@gmail.com

Austen Inspired

The Parson of Pemberley

No Promise of the Kind

Mr. Darcy's Brides

Spells Spoken Lightly

Darcy & Lizzy

Mr. Darcy's Good Opinion

Mr. Darcy's Debt

Mr. Darcy Properly Humbled

Clever Compromises

Christian Fiction/Romance

Cassidy Jane

Courting Cassidy Jane

Wedding Cassidy Jane

26629617R00176

Printed in Poland
by Amazon Fulfillment
Poland Sp. z o.o., Wrocław